W9-AVB-206

Thomas S. Parrott Memorial Library
St. Albans School
Washington, D. C.

LEIF THE UNLUCKY

Leif the unlucky

Erik Christian Haugaard

Houghton Mifflin Company

Boston 1982

Thomas S. Parrott Memorial Library
St. Albans School
Washington, D. C.

The author wishes to thank the Ministry of Greenland for the help and support that made this book possible.

Library of Congress Cataloging in Publication Data
Haugaard, Erik Christian.
Leif the unlucky.

Summary: Faced with increasingly harsh winters and deteriorating morale in fifteenth-century Greenland, a young man struggles to rally the last few surviving Norse colonists, who feel their only hope is rescue by ships from Norway.
1. Greenland—History—Juvenile fiction.
[1. Greenland—History—Fiction] I. Title.
PZ7 .H286Le   [Fic]   82-1053
ISBN 0-395-32156-5   AACR2

Copyright © 1982 by Erik Christian Haugaard
Map copyright © 1982 by Brian Lalor

All rights reserved. No part of this work may be reproduced or transmitted in any form or by any means, electronic or mechanical, including photocopying and recording, or by any information storage or retrieval system, except as may be expressly permitted by the 1976 Copyright Act or in writing by the publisher. Requests for permission should be addressed in writing to Houghton Mifflin Company, 2 Park St., Boston, Massachusetts 02108.

Printed in the United States of America

v 10 9 8 7 6 5 4 3 2 1

F
H

For Myrna

8511

Contents

Foreword

IN THE year 986 a fleet of longships, under the command of Erik the Red, left Iceland, setting their course for Greenland. The weather was bad, storms and headwinds split the fleet, and only fourteen ships arrived at their destination, Eriksfjord.

Thus began the Norsemen's colonization of that huge ice-covered island — in tragedy. It was to end the same way. But in between, right to the end of the thirteenth century, they managed well enough, for their houses were substantial and they built sixteen churches. At one time they numbered more than five thousand people. They even had a bishop of Greenland, who lived in Gardar and had room in his stables for a hundred cows.

In the fourteenth century the weather conditions changed, the climate grew colder, and the cows and horses could no longer survive. Ill luck haunted the colony, for in Norway, the country to which they had submitted voluntarily, political conditions grew unstable. No ships were sent to that far-off place, to which the pope had given the name "the end of the world." There were still bishops of Greenland, but the title was now empty and those who held it never left Norway. Troubles and poverty could be found at home, there was no need to seek them in such dangerous waters as those around Greenland.

In 1406 a ship set sail from Norway to Iceland. Blown off course, it landed in Greenland. The crew stayed four winters among their fellow Norsemen there before returning to Iceland in 1410. This is the last documented contact with the unlucky colony.

What happened to them we shall never know. We have found their graves, the ruins of their houses and churches, but the true tale of their tragic end will never be told. In *Leif the Unlucky* I have guessed at it, tried to imagine what might have happened. It is a story for a dark December evening, a winter's tale.

Erik Christian Haugaard
Toad Hall   September 30, 1981

LEIF THE UNLUCKY

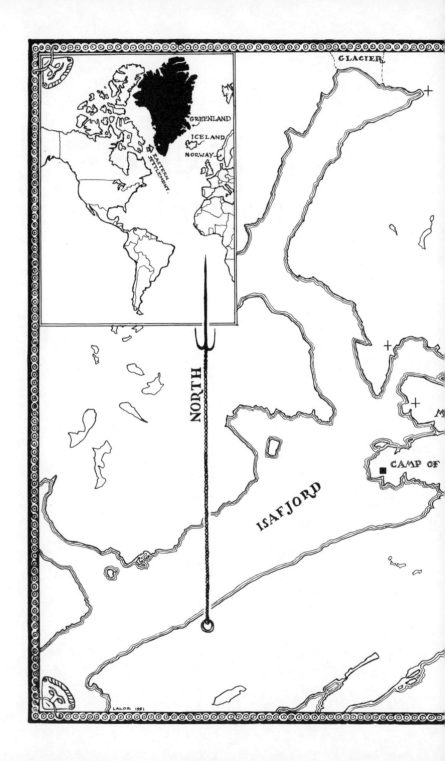

GLACIER

GREENLAND

ICELAND

NORWAY

EASTERN SETTLEMENT

NORTH

ISAFJORD

CAMP OF

M

LALOR 1981

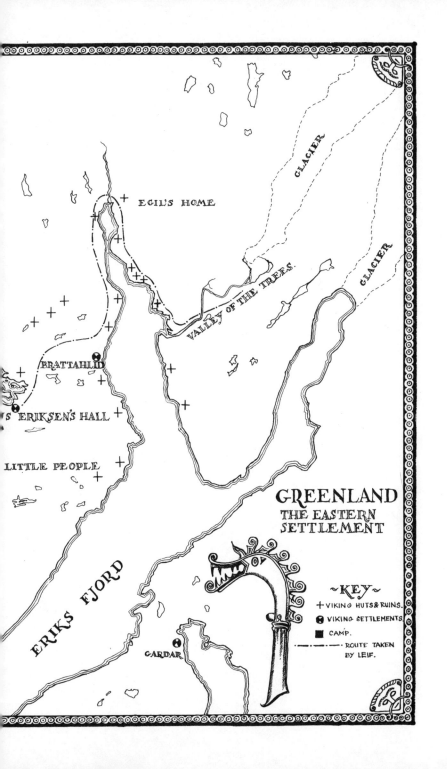

GLACIER

GLACIER

EGIL'S HOME

VALLEY OF THE TREES

BRATTAHLID

ERIKSEN'S HALL

LITTLE PEOPLE

GREENLAND
THE EASTERN
SETTLEMENT

ERIKS FJORD

GARDAR

~KEY~
+ VIKING HUTS & RUINS.
◓ VIKING SETTLEMENTS
■ CAMP.
— · — · — ROUTE TAKEN
BY LEIF.

1

The Boy

WHEN THE boy climbed to the pass of the low mountain range that divides Eriksfjord from Isafjord, he sat down on a rock. It was a warm summer day. Flowers bloomed among the grass, and below him, in the blue waters of Eriksfjord, a lonely iceberg sailed. From up here Brattahlid looked as it must have when all the Norsemen of Greenland gathered to discuss and settle their affairs. Then, on the stony beaches, boat after boat would be drawn up to lie like fat seals basking in the sun. Laughing youths would play games of strength, while the older men would watch, remembering — and perhaps regretting — what they had lost. Then, the Norsemen could be counted in thousands; now they were only a few hundred and almost all the boats that once had cleaved the waters of the fjord were wrecked and gone.

But the boy was not thinking of those days, although

they had been as filled with promise as his own were with despair. He was dreaming of a time even before that: before the farm of Brattahlid had been built, before the white god Christ had come to Greenland. When he closed his eyes he could see, for a moment, the fifteen longships of Erik the Red sailing up the fjord, as they had five hundred years ago. O to have lived then! he thought, imagining himself standing in the bow of that great chieftain's ship.

From where the boy sat the large hall, the church, and even the farm buildings of Brattahlid appeared solid enough to hold off wind and weather for several centuries more. But he knew that some of the buildings were mere ruins, while others, including the church, were badly in need of repairs that would never be made.

The boy was fifteen — strong, squarely built, and tall for his age. He wore a woolen tunic that ended above the knees. Around his waist was a sealskin belt from which dangled his most valuable possession, a knife in a sheath made from the antler of a reindeer. His hair was blond with a reddish tinge, it fell to his shoulders and curled. His name was Leif Magnusson; and he was the son of Magnus Eriksen, who had one of the four farms on the shores of Isafjord that were still inhabited.

A figure entered the church, which was once the pride of Brattahlid. Although the boy was too far away to recognize who it was, he felt certain that it was his mother's cousin, Olaf. Some — among them Olaf's older brother, Gunner Ulfson — called him Olaf the Lame, for he had been born with a clubfoot. But it was as if God, feeling sorry for him, had decided to give him beauty as a birthgift as well, for surely Olaf was handsome. His body was long and slender, his forehead arched and his chin strong, his hair curly and black, his nose narrow and slightly curved, but most remarkable of all were his eyes. Soft and deep brown, in those rare moments when he grew angry they could turn black.

As long as anyone could remember, there had been no priest at Brattahlid — nor, for that matter, anywhere else in Greenland. Once, long ago in Gardar on Einersfjord, a bishop had resided; he had been so rich, it was told, that he had a hundred cows in his barn. Then, the black-clothed priests were to be seen everywhere. But the bishop died and no new one came from Norway. The priests followed their lord, and finally the last of God's servants was laid to rest.

If God could be served only by those who had been ordained his priests, then he was servantless now. But Olaf had appointed himself to the vacant position, and proved a most willing servant. The Latin he mumbled came from a breviary found in the bishop's house in Gardar; yet it must be admitted that Olaf did not know the meaning of the words he loved to declaim. He thought of them as formulae that could cure sickness in both man and beast.

Leif got up from the rock. For a moment he stood

perfectly still, his hand resting on the hilt of his knife. He listened to the sound coming from a brook, as its waters rushed over a small cliff and fell in a miniature waterfall onto the stones and pebbles below. Then, as if he had heard some message in the song of the little stream, he shook his head and started down the path to Brattahlid.

A flock of sheep and a few goats were grazing near the hall. As the boy approached the sheep ran away, but one of the goats came up to him, bleating loudly. It was pure white and wore a collar of braided leather. Leif recognized it as the pet of Ingeborg, Olaf's niece and the daughter of Gunner Ulfson, master of Brattahlid. Although Leif's mother and Gunner were cousins, she seldom visited her kinsman's hall. "At Brattahlid," she would say, "guests have to dine on the steam from Gunner's soup kettle."

The boy scratched the goat's head between its horns while he looked about for its mistress. He was fond of Ingeborg and it was she he had come to see. She was a frail girl, so tiny when she was born that no one at Brattahlid had thought she would live. But she had survived, and her uncle Olaf thought that he was the cause of this miracle, for on the bone of a goat he had engraved two Latin words of great power — *Exaudi Deus* — and hidden it in her cradle.

Since the girl was nowhere to be seen and Leif had no wish to meet her father, he walked to the church. The entrance was so low that a tall man had to stoop to go inside. The door had lost its hinges long ago and was left permanently ajar. The walls had once been covered with paneling, but that had been removed and used to repair a boat, even before the last priest had died. Now, with its stark, rough stone walls, the building more resembled the grave-chamber of a heathen king than a temple to Christ.

In the twilight of the room Leif could see Olaf kneeling in front of the altar, a large square stone. On it were two bronze candlesticks, but it was a hundred years since candles had been placed in them. Now a small stone lamp that burned tallow was the only illumination, and it was only lighted when Olaf conducted a service.

"Ad vesperas antiphona . . ." Olaf's voice droned, as he read from the top of the page to the bottom, without seeming to betray that he had no knowledge of what he muttered. He had been taught the alphabet when he was very young by a very old man who, in turn, had been taught it as a child by the last priest in Brattahlid. Leif had no such learning. The scrawls in the book meant nothing to him, although he did not doubt that they had great magical powers, especially the first letter, which the monks had ornamented in colors.

"Olaf!" Leif whispered.

The cripple put the book down between the candlesticks and turned to see who had interrupted his devotion. When he saw the boy he smiled, raised both hands, and blessed him.

Silently, as if there were some agreement between

them that the church was not the right place to talk, they walked outside. "What is new from Isafjord?" Olaf asked. The bright sunlight made him squint for a moment.

"Nothing. I have cut the grass in the meadow and, if it doesn't rain, we shall have enough hay for both sheep and goats this winter. But tell me, Olaf, how does one make iron? Our sickle is so worn, it will not last much longer, and look —" Leif drew his knife, its blade worn thin from having been sharpened too many times. "I know that once iron was melted at Brattahlid."

"In my grandfather's time there was a smithy; then they could easily have made you a new sickle." Olaf glanced about him as if he expected to find the forge if he looked hard enough. "Then, the walls of the church were covered with pictures of God and all his angels."

Leif nodded, he had heard his mother's cousin speak many times before about those pictures. "Do you think that there is anyone left in Greenland who knows how to make iron?" he asked.

"They say" — Olaf paused and looked cunningly at Leif — "they say the monks who lived in Ketilsfjord knew the art."

"But they have been dead a hundred years or more." Leif smiled. "I don't think they will be any more help to me than Ketil himself — whoever he was."

"He sailed with Erik the Red!" Olaf prided himself on knowing the history of the Norsemen in Greenland, although in truth he knew little of it, and no matter what ancient name was mentioned he would say that it belonged to one of the companions of Erik the Red.

"If one collected all the old iron one could find, how could one melt it down?" the boy asked, putting the question more to himself than to his cousin.

"It would take more heat than to cook soup," Olaf answered slyly.

"If we don't get iron we shall have no soup to cook," Leif replied. "How will we cut grass to get hay for winter without knives?"

"A ship will come!" Olaf threw up his arms to give emphasis to what he was saying. "It will come from the king of Norway! It will bring a new bishop to Greenland, who will rebuild the churches!" Olaf looked out over the fjord, shading his eyes with his hand to see better, but all that sailed on the blue waters was a green iceberg with a peak that pointed toward the heavens.

"The only ship that I know of came to Herjolfness, down in the south." Leif turned to look at his cousin. "They sacked the church and took some of the people away as slaves!"

"But that wasn't a longship," Olaf argued. "It was manned by people who spoke a language no one understood. They were evil men!" Somehow the moment Olaf said this the strangers — who had raided the small colony at Herjolfness and taken away with them everything of value — ceased to be of importance. Now he could return to his favorite daydream, in which a fine royal longship would sail up Eriksfjord, its scarlet sail decorated with the cross of Christ and, on board, priests and a new bishop for Gardar who would bring back the glory of God to Greenland.

This ship of the king of Norway had sailed in Leif's dreams as well; but his ship had contained not priests and bishops, but warriors with shields and shiny swords. Yet of late he had begun to hate these dreams. There were even moments when he thought that the people of Greenland deserved no better than to be taken away as slaves. On his way down from the pass Leif had had a good look at the hayfields; only on one had the grass been cut, and this had not been turned, so that already it was mildewed.

"Did you know that Sigurd Ivarson and his children have come to live at Brattahlid?" Olaf hesitated, but when the boy did not reply, he continued, "They came yesterday. Sigurd said that he found it too lonesome now that his wife is dead."

Another farm abandoned, Leif thought; soon there will only be Norsemen at Brattahlid, Isafjord, and Gardar. He tried to reckon how many that would be, but he gave up. "Has Sigurd any sheep left?" he asked aloud, remembering that he had once gone with his father to visit Sigurd; the farm was a lonely one at the end of Eriksfjord.

"Gunner has gone back with him to get the sheep.

Tomorrow they will row down there in Gunner's boat and bring back whatever else there is of value." Olaf smiled thinly. "I am sure there is not much."

Leif nodded. "It is best we all live close to each other." He remembered Sigurd as a little gray man who had no faith in himself; his wife had had strength for two. He will be no gain for the people of Brattahlid, he thought. Sigurd Ivarson was known to be lazy, a man who would do no work unless driven to it by hunger or a whip.

"Where is Ingeborg?" The boy lowered his voice almost to a whisper when he said the girl's name, which made the handsome cripple smile.

"There she is!" Olaf pointed toward the beach. The goat had found her and she was walking toward them with one arm around her pet's neck.

As Leif ran down to meet the daughter of the master of Brattahlid he noticed that she was barefoot and that her dress was darned in several places. A hundred years ago, he thought, she would have been taken for a servant, and, in the times of Erik the Red, for a slave.

2

The Girl

SOME PEOPLE walk as if they want to plant their feet
deep into the earth, leaving footprints for all the
world to see and admire. But there are others who step
so lightly that they hardly bend the blades of grass. Ingeborg Gudrinsdaughter did not take after her father,
she resembled her mother, Gudrin, who in her short life
had walked lightly on the earth. Everything about the
girl was delicate and Leif always felt gross and clumsy
when he was near her. He thought, though he never
told her, that she was like the little flowers of Greenland
that burst forth from the frozen earth in spring and
blossom during the short summer.

Although Leif's thoughts about Ingeborg were as soft
as the southern breeze, he often spoke harshly to hide
them. The words he left unspoken were always kind,
but those his tongue formed were often awkward and
sometimes unkind. Now, as soon as he met her, he asked,

"Why have you not cut the hay in the upper meadows?" And the tone of his voice would have made anyone believe that it was Ingeborg, not her father, he held responsible for this neglect.

"My father says that there will be hay enough from the meadows down by the hall." Ingeborg smiled. "And you, have you been haymaking?"

"I have" — Leif paused and then added shyly — "had much to do." This was true, for he and some other youngsters had done most of the work on his father's farm that spring. It was as if all the Norsemen in Greenland had caught some strange sickness, which tapped not only their courage but their strength as well, leaving them to sit by their fires like toothless old men and women, waiting for death. The winters seemed to grow longer and harder. It was as if the sun no longer had the power to give warmth, even in summer. Some said God himself had deserted the little colony on this land at the end of the world, and so there was no longer any point in continuing to struggle.

"My father has been fishing," Ingeborg said, to excuse his not having cut the grass in the upper meadows.

"And how much did he catch?" Leif glanced toward the place where the high, triangular wooden construction for drying fish once stood. The previous winter Gunner Ulfson had cut it down and used it for firewood.

Ingeborg, who had followed his gaze, blushed guiltily. "My father is drying the fish in the hut over there," she said, pointing to a hovel with a half-sunken roof.

"He can't, the fish will rot in there and won't be fit for feeding the dogs," Leif remarked contemptuously. "It would have been better if he had strung them between two rocks. Fish need sun and air to dry properly."

"That is what he did." Ingeborg laughed. "But the wind blew them down and the dogs ate the fish before we noticed what had happened." The girl looked out over the fjord and her face took on the same dreamlike expression that had graced Olaf's. "My father says that next year, for sure, the king of Norway will send a ship. All we have to do is hold out until then; and we have enough sheep for another winter."

"The sheep of Brattahlid must have gone bald, since the daughter of its chieftain is dressed in rags," Leif said, adding grimly, "The ships have never come, but winter always has. Someday when the nights grow long and cold we will have no more sheep to kill and no tallow for our lamps, and then . . . then . . ." Leif shook his head, not daring to continue the sentence.

Two tears formed in Ingeborg's eyes and rolled down her cheeks. She cried not because she was afraid of dying, but because the boy had accused her of wearing rags.

Leif saw her tears, but he misunderstood their source. "But it need not come to that." He held up his hand, as if arguing with someone who he feared might interrupt him. "We must change. It's not only that we must work harder, but we must try to live like the little people from the north. We must hunt more, especially the seal. Those boats that are supposed to come from the king of Norway," he continued almost angrily, "are like the dreams of children. When children close their eyes they can hunt and kill the mighty white bear, and yet when they are awake they can be frightened of a fox."

"Why do you think the ship will never come?" Ingeborg asked sadly.

"Surely it would have come long ago. Neither your father, nor mine, nor anyone alive on Greenland has ever seen a ship of the king of Norway." Leif looked at Ingeborg and then laughed. "Maybe there never was a king of Norway!"

"My father has a small chest filled with silver coins of the king of Norway. Have not all of us, hundreds of years ago, come from Iceland and Norway? Are we not Norse?" the girl demanded.

"Oh yes, that is all true; once, no doubt, the king did send his ships to Greenland. But don't you understand" — Leif's voice was very earnest — "we must forget that now; at least, not think so much about it. We are dream-worn, and if we don't wake we shall die! We can live here." Leif's hand swept the air, taking in the whole landscape. "Do you think that Erik the Red, when he set sail with fifteen ships, thought that the king of Norway would one day have to come to cut the grass for him or bait the hooks for his line?"

"It was warmer then, my father says. They had cows, milk and butter and cheese."

"It might have been warmer then," Leif agreed. "But is that a good enough reason for giving up now? Each year you eat more sheep than you have lambs, your flock will be smaller."

"What do you want us to do?" Ingeborg's voice quavered.

"I would like all the Norsemen in Greenland to come here to Brattahlid or Isafjord, bringing whatever sheep or goats they have left." Leif spoke slowly, for this was a plan he had long thought about. "Then when we are many, people will regain their courage, for 'man delights in man,' so it says in the sagas. The men will hunt and fish together and women will spin and weave again. In the long winter nights we will try to remember the tales of our great-grandfathers and tell them to each other."

"And you will sit in the chieftain's chair: Earl Leif the Lucky!" Ingeborg laughed.

"By the time I can grow a beard there won't be anyone left to lead." Leif laughed as well. "I'll tell you what we should do, Ingeborg — steal your father's boat and sail to Iceland." This was a dream the boy had dreamed both when he was asleep and when he was awake. Gunner Ulfson's boat was twenty feet long. Although small, it was built like a longship. Once it had had both mast and sail, but Gunner had found other uses for them. It was the last of the boats in Brattahlid; when it was gone they would not even be able to row across the fjord and visit those who were still alive in Gardar.

"My father says that she cannot sail far from land. She leaks so badly that it takes two men to bail her to keep her from sinking."

"She could be repaired." Again the voice of the boy sounded as if he were blaming Ingeborg for the state of her father's possessions, but this time he recognized it and quickly softened his tone. "We have a wrecked boat at Isafjord, but there are still a few good planks in her; between the two, we could make one seaworthy boat. Do you think your father would let me try this winter?"

"You know my father." Ingeborg blushed with shame. "Whatever he has in his hands he never lets go of."

"Except all of Brattahlid!" Suddenly all the fury the boy felt against the grownups, who stood between him and his plans, rose like a whale from the water. "Gunner Ulfson has not even turned the grass he cut. It is covered with mildew!" Leif shouted as he kicked a small stone, sending it flying in the direction of the hall. "He wants to be master of Brattahlid, chieftain over us all, but he will do nothing to save us! Nothing! He sits and gloats while he counts the silver of the king of Norway, which is as useful here as that stone." Leif glanced down, aimed his foot at another pebble, and kicked it.

"They say that you have made yourself chieftain of the boys on Isafjord and they obey you as if you were an earl."

The boy looked toward the low hills that separated him from his home. There was some truth in what Ingeborg said but suddenly, without knowing why, he did not want to admit it. "Since my father is like yours and will not attend to his farm, someone else must do it."

"Look, here comes Gunner!" Ingeborg pointed south to where four figures had just emerged above a ridge. Two of them were children. "There are a couple of housecarls for your hird." She laughed.

"One of them is a girl," Leif corrected.

"You have sharp eyes if you can see that from here." Ingeborg raised her hand to her forehead and shaded her gaze.

"Oh, I can't," Leif replied. "But I know that Sigurd Ivarson has a daughter as well as a son."

"Then she can weave and spin for you," Ingeborg teased. "Or do you have girls in your hird?"

"I don't have a hird, but if I did, why not? There were several women who sailed with Leif to Vineland." The boy's cheeks were burning, for it was his wish to gather a group of children round himself like the chieftains in the sagas; in the old times such a group had been called a hird. Leif felt foolish, as if he had been caught playing by a grownup; he was, after all, fifteen years old. "I must go home," he said urgently and turned toward the hills as if he were going to run all the way.

"Come again soon." Ingeborg held out her hand and Leif took it. "I am glad," she said, "that you do allow women in your hird." Then, laughing and blushing at the same time, she reminded him that it was not far from Isafjord to Brattahlid.

3

The Spear

WHERE HAVE you been, boy?" Magnus Eriksen shouted, noticing with irritation that his son was almost as tall as himself. "Have you been to Brattahlid again?"

"I have," Leif replied. He was looking out at Isafjord, which was packed with icebergs, wondering whether it was true that in the time of Erik the Red much less of the land had been covered by ice and that none of the three glaciers that now emptied themselves into the waters had been there. The icebergs were different colors: blue, green, crystal, and in the middle was one that was black. They were beautiful, but the boy who had looked at these giant floating islands of ice all of his life did not think so, he preferred the open waters of Eriksfjord.

"To get an answer out of you is like dragging a fish

Thomas S. Parrott Memorial Library
St. Albans School
Washington, D. C.

8511

from the sea." Magnus was leaning against the ruin of a cowbarn, part of which still could be used for storing hay. Suddenly he smiled. "Tell me, did you see Gunner Ulfson? What is the news from Brattahlid?"

"Sigurd Ivarson has given up his farm and has come to stay with Gunner." Leif knew that this news would interest his father.

"Three more mouths to feed, three more bellies to fill. Gunner won't get any work out of Sigurd unless he takes a stick to him, as they say Solveig used to." Magnus laughed, he did not care for his wife's cousin.

"The boy is no child and neither is the girl; they may be of more use to Gunner than Sigurd himself."

"Do you think the daughter favors her mother?" Magnus looked at his son keenly while he waited for an answer.

"I don't know. I did not see her, except from a great distance. They were just returning to Brattahlid with their sheep when I left." Leif knew that it would irritate his father to know that Sigurd had not come empty-handed to Gunner.

Magnus Eriksen narrowed his eyes. "How many sheep?"

"I told you I was too far away to count them," Leif answered, while he thought, How grasping my father is!

"Half a hundred?" Magnus demanded, still squinting as was his habit when he was angry; the thought of

Gunner Ulfson getting fifty fat sheep for nothing made him furious.

Leif smiled and in the hope of getting his father into a better humor said, "Although I don't know exactly how many there were, I think there were less than twenty. I was told that Gunner believes that the king of Norway will surely send a ship next year. The master of Brattahlid spends his days counting his silver and dreams at night how he is going to spend it once he arrives in Norway."

"How does he know the ship will come? Has he had any omens?" Magnus glanced eagerly out over the fjord. "Yesterday I saw five ravens flying from the south; they were not ordinary birds of flesh and feathers. Gunner may be right!"

"And how many people predicted last summer that the ship would come this summer?" Leif shrugged his shoulders in disgust. "And two years ago, didn't Gunner send his boat to Gardar because he dreamt that the ship had already come there?"

"They flew — those ravens — in a straight line, one after another like an arrow in the sky. I have never seen ravens fly in that manner before." Magnus shook his head in wonder. "If the ships should come and take us all back to Norway I think we shall not arrive as beggars."

Leif glanced at his father's face, but looked quickly away. He felt ashamed of what he had seen in his features. Magnus Eriksen and Gunner Ulfson had many things in common and chief among them was a liking for silver. Both guarded their little stores of wealth as if they were princely treasures.

"Has anyone turned the hay in the upper pasture?" Leif asked.

"I told Sven to do it, but whether he has or not I don't know." Magnus was lying, for he had given no such order to his servant, but he was the kind of man who almost believed in his own lies as soon as he had uttered them.

Leif knew only too well his father's weaknesses and asked pointedly, "Shall I ask Sven if he has done it?"

"If he hasn't, tell him to do it tomorrow." This was as near an admission of guilt as Magnus could come. "If the weather keeps up we shall have more hay than we need," he added.

"We shall sell hay to Gunner Ulfson come spring. He will need it," Leif explained. "They have cut the grass only in the fields near the hall and they have let the sheep graze in the upper meadow."

"By spring, if they don't want to slaughter all of their animals, they will have to buy hay from me." The thought of getting his hands on some of Gunner's silver made Magnus smile, he felt as if he were counting it already.

"If that should happen," Leif said, "then ask for his boat."

"It is a hundred years old and worthless." Magnus sniffed with contempt.

"It may be even older than that, and I am sure that in Norway, where every mountain is covered with trees, it would be judged worthless, but here it is still a boat." As Leif spoke he realized that he was talking in vain, his father would sell their hay for worthless silver coins. Yet he could not help arguing. "Here in Greenland, Father, a boat, hay, even a plank of wood or the blade of a scythe are our coins. Those bits of silver of yours are useless here, it is only in Norway that they have any value!"

"But the ship will come! An old woman who lived in a hut in the innermost part of the fjord, where the glacier meets the sea and the icebergs are born, told my mother at my birth that I would sit beside the king of Norway." Dreamily Magnus Eriksen stared out over the fjord. He did not see the blue-green water packed with icebergs; he saw himself proudly entering the hall of the king of Norway.

The boy turned from his father. Under his breath Leif muttered, "Fool . . . fool . . . fool . . ." And when he was far enough away that his voice could not be heard by Magnus he screamed it out loud — "Fool!" — and stamped the ground as hard as he could.

The two largest farms on Isafjord were located on a small bay almost enclosed by a headland: the one nearest the shore belonged to the boy's father, the other to

Ravn Eriksen, Magnus's brother. Ravn was the older by nearly ten years; a childless widower, he lived alone, except for his servant, Kark, whom he treated as a slave or a friend according to his mood. He took no interest in his farm; each summer Kark cut just enough grass to furnish hay for their flock of goats whose milk and meat kept the two men alive.

The grass in his father's meadow had not been turned, which did not surprise Leif. Since he did not wish to go home, it occurred to him that he could visit his uncle Ravn and ask him if he knew the secret of making iron. Although the boy judged his father and Gunner Ulfson harshly for neglecting their farms, he felt no such anger against his uncle.

Ravn Eriksen's hall had been built to house a chieftain and its bare stone walls had once been covered by timber paneling. All that remained of this former splendor were the two great carved beams that formed part of the chieftain's chair and rose to support the very roof of the building. They were ancient, from those times when Odin and Thor were still worshipped; in almost all of the halls in Greenland these reminders of the old gods had been destroyed.

A low fire was smoldering on the hearth, the smoke was rising lazily toward the hole in the roof but enough of it stayed below to make the boy's eyes smart. In the twilight of the hall he could see nothing and was about to leave when his uncle called to him.

"Why does Leif Magnusson honor his uncle's hall? Has he come to listen to an old man's secrets, the wisdom of his years?" Ravn Eriksen laughed. He and Kark were sitting on the floor. Between them, where the sunlight that shone through the smoke-hole in the roof touched the floor, was a chess board.

"Take it away," the master commanded and as he stood up he gave the board a slight shove so that the pieces fell in disarray.

"I have come to ask you how to make iron," Leif said, watching Kark collect the small carved figures and place them in a box. "But I am disturbing you?"

"Go, and attend to the goats," Ravn ordered as he took the little wooden chest from Kark's hand and put it on the table. Then he seated himself in the chieftain's chair and, with a wave of his hand, invited Leif to sit down on the bench beside him.

"Not at all, you are most welcome," Ravn Eriksen said and glanced toward the door to see whether Kark had gone. Satisfied that the servant had done his bidding, he leaned forward and whispered as if he were telling an important secret, "You see, I was losing." Then he sat back and said aloud, "When I was a boy, I could not bear not to win; if I lost in any game I would lose my temper as well, which did not really matter since I had more than enough to spare. My grandfather told me that with age I would learn how to bear it. He was wrong, I still hate losing, which proves that the advice of the old is seldom right." Ravn Eriksen laughed loudly in appreciation of his own wit. Suddenly he stopped abruptly and said in a normal tone of voice, "As for ironmaking, I would not know how to go about it. They once had a smithy at Brattahlid, but that had already disappeared when I was a child. There is iron here, 'bog ore' my grandfather called it. I wonder if Kark would know how to melt it down? The monks on Ketilsfjord knew the art."

"So Olaf Ulfson told me." The boy laughed. "But they have been dead a hundred years. Maybe I should go there and dig up one of their skulls and ask it to help me."

"You'll get as much sense from a dead monk as from a live Olaf. Have you asked your father or Gunner? Not that either of them would know anything of much use to anyone."

"They are waiting for the ship from the king of Norway to come," Leif said with a grin. "My father told me that an old woman who lived in a hut at the end of Isafjord had foretold that he was destined to dine with kings."

Ravn Eriksen laughed long and loudly. "Old mother Hildegun she was called. She lived in a hut not far from the glacier. Some people say that she had not even been washed at birth, but that may be untrue. I can tell you that when I knew her, she stank worse than a billy goat. She looked so old that you could have believed she came to Greenland with Erik the Red. When she died about twenty winters ago people said that the devil had come to take her. If that's true, he has strange taste . . . Did your father tell you what she had prophesied for me?"

"No." Leif shook his head.

"Somehow I didn't think he would." Ravn Eriksen started to laugh so heartily that he could hardly speak. "She said . . . she said that I would become . . . pope!" he finally uttered, while tears ran from his eyes. "She was touched! As mad as anyone could be. My grandfather said that her family had always had weak heads. But she came of good stock on her mother's side, for her great-great-great-grandfather was the very Ketil whom the fjord is called after."

"Will the ship ever come?" Leif asked. Suddenly, the boy was aware that he did not want his uncle to agree that the ship of the king of Norway would never arrive in Greenland.

"It could come," Ravn said slowly. "There must be people alive other places than here." With his finger he drew a line in the dust that covered the top of the table. "Maybe they have had bad years in Norway, too. Summers when the hay would not dry and winters that came too soon. Maybe they have had wars. Or maybe they have had the sicknesses that we have had here." Leif's uncle paused and looked at the boy, then he made more marks on the table. "But the ship won't come for your sake or your father's or Gunner Ulfson's. Nor will they come to make me pope. They will come for a reason that we don't even know. Whether we live or die means nothing to the king of Norway. I think they have forgotten us."

Ravn studied the lines he had drawn in the dirt of the table as if they were meaningful. "You see, we do not appear in the dreams of that king, though he is part of our dreams — of Gunner's, your father's, and my dreams too, I suppose. We have nothing left to do but dream."

Ravn sighed and, putting his hand on top of the boy's, pressed it gently. "It is hard for one as young as you to be born to the fate of the old, whose dreams always turn to the past because the future only holds the grave."

"But that is not true!" Leif almost shouted. "I will not dream, for dreams sap your strength," he declared.

"Without dreams, my boy" — his uncle smiled kindly as he spoke — "we would have hanged ourselves from the rafters long ago." Then, as if he had suddenly discovered the fact, he said, "But you have almost come of age and need the grownups' playthings!" Ravn Eriksen rose and walked to a dark corner of the room.

He returned carrying a spear. "Your great-great-grandfather brought this from Norway. Take it, I no longer have any use for it."

Leif's fingers slid along the smooth shaft of the weapon; its head was still untarnished. He stood up. Weighing it in his hand he felt the perfect balance of the spear. "Thank you," he muttered and then more loudly, to show he appreciated the gift, he said, "I shall bring no shame on it."

This last statement made his uncle laugh, though not unkindly. "My boy," he began, "the only weapons that know no shame are those which have never been used. Your great-great-grandfather was known as a trouble-maker wherever he went. Run along and play with your toy."

When Leif was gone Ravn Eriksen went to the door of his house and called in a loud voice for his servant and friend, "Kark! Kark!"

4

Greta Helgasdaughter

A SWORD or a spear is a dead thing, it has neither breath nor life, nor the power to take away warmth from the live flesh of a man unless it is wielded by the arm of a warrior. Yet it is often given a name and human qualities, which could make one believe that such a weapon had a soul given to it when it was formed in the blacksmith's fiery furnace. As the hand grasps the hilt of a sword or the shaft of a spear, a strange feeling of power seems to pass from the weapon through the arm into the heart and brain of the man who holds it.

Leif felt this as he seized the shaft of the spear worn smooth by kinsmen's hands. Once he was far enough away from the hall of Ravn Eriksen not to be seen, Leif lifted the weapon high in the air as if he wanted to show it to the sun, the mountains, and all the world. But a moment later he recalled his uncle's words and then he felt ashamed. For Leif, too, knew that his great-great-grandfather had been declared an outlaw in Iceland. He had killed a man there and that was why he had come to Greenland. He had been called Thorkild the Bold, but some said that "brute" would have been a more fitting name. Thorkild had been one of the last Norsemen to settle in Greenland. He married Ragnhild Thorasdaughter and she, who claimed as her ancestor Erik the Red, discoverer of Greenland and the first chieftain of Brattahlid, was Leif's great-great-grandmother.

The boy sat down on a large rock to examine the spear. The blade was made of iron, polished smooth and still sharp. At the other end of the weapon was a bronze knob fashioned in the shape of a dragon's head; this not only served as a decoration but helped to balance the weapon as well. Finally Leif noticed that runic letters had been cut into the shaft, but he could not read them.

He took the weapon to a hut that the children of the settlement called their "hall." It had long been abandoned, and its roof was only waiting for a winter storm to cave it in. There under some tattered skins he hid the spear, for he did not want his father to know he had it, for fear he might take it away from him.

One of the great pleasures of ownership lies in showing that which we treasure to others, and in this Leif did not differ from anyone else. He went to look for Bjarne and Odd, the sons of his father's servant, with whom he had been brought up.

Bjarne had been born in the same year and month as

Leif, both were children of the spring. Bjarne was shorter and broader and probably stronger than Leif, but this possibility never entered his mind. Such was his admiration for his master's son that Bjarne would have felt it a disloyalty to be his superior in any way.

Odd was one year older than Bjarne and Leif, and when one is so young a year can contain a great deal of experience. But it was not only the difference in age that set him apart from the other boys at Isafjord. He was a strange, secretive youngster who seemed happiest in his own company and not in need of friends. Odd would often disappear for weeks and when he returned offer no explanation of why he had gone away or where he had been. Leif was a little in awe of him and Bjarne was torn between admiration and jealousy of his older brother. Leif often felt that Odd's gaze was more critical than approving, and would ask the older boy what he was thinking. Odd seldom answered, most often he just smiled and shook his head.

Leif found the two boys together by the fjord, fishing. Luck had been with them, there on the rocks next to them were six large fish. Leif joined them silently. He wanted very much to show Bjarne his spear but he also wanted it to appear as if he thought the weapon of not too great importance. A strong rope is woven from many lesser strings, and such was Leif's character that pride certainly played a part in it.

"I have been to Brattahlid," he began. "Sigurd Ivarson has given up his farm and has come to stay there with his children."

"Last year your father bought two ewes from him." Bjarne looked eagerly at Leif. "Remember, Sigurd brought them here and his son, Egil, was with him. I did not care much for him."

"Sigurd or Egil?"

"The two of them." Bjarne turned to watch Odd drawing in the line, he had caught a fish. "To curry favor with your father, Sigurd spoke ill of Gunner Ulfson; then nothing at Brattahlid suited him."

"My father must have enjoyed that, just as speaking ill of us must please Gunner Ulfson's ears." Now Leif was looking at the older boy. "And what about you, Odd, did you like them?"

Odd grabbed the large sea trout by the gills and, carefully removing the hook, which was of bone, he twisted the head of the fish backward until its neck was broken, then threw it alongside the rest of his catch. "We would catch more fish if we had stronger lines," he said hesitantly, "and iron hooks."

"But we don't have any!" It irritated Leif that Odd so often complained of the very things that dissatisfied him, too. "We must make do with what we have," he said almost sharply.

"Then we shall have to make do with Egil and his father as well." Odd grinned as if he had said something witty.

"Let's take the fish up to the hall, I have something I want to show you." Leif picked up the largest of the fish and the other two boys took the rest.

"What is it?" Bjarne asked, but Leif merely looked up at the sky mysteriously and remarked that "it" was at the "hall."

When they delivered the fish Leif's mother called him inside to hear news of her cousin Gunner Ulfson. Greta Helgasdaughter was a thin woman more used to uttering bitter words than sweet ones. Within her she contained a rage against her fate, which had dried her up. It was as if a fire burned where her heart should have been. Leif felt more fear than love for his mother.

When she heard the news of Sigurd Ivarson's arrival at Brattahlid she laughed and interrupted her son. "When we were young Gunner never liked him. Now if it had been Sigurd who had died, then he would truly have bid Solveig welcome to his hall. He used to run after her like a hound after a bitch."

Leif looked away; he had inherited from some unknown ancestor — for certainly neither his father nor his mother had this trait — a natural delicacy that was easily offended. He wondered for a moment what his mother had been like as a girl. She could not have been like Ingeborg, or could she? Because he was thinking of Ingeborg he asked, "What was Gudrin like?"

"Gudrin?" His mother repeated the word as if she could not recall anyone by that name.

"Ingeborg's mother," he explained.

"And Gunner Ulfson's wife." Greta Helgasdaughter laughed and Leif could not help but notice how little joy there was in his mother's laughter. "Gudrin was as pure as the water that melts from the glaciers; to mix her with Gunner, who already resembled the still water of a soggy swamp, was hardly kind to her. My uncle should have found some sow for him, they could have wallowed in the same filth . . . Gudrin was fool enough to obey her father, and she was sold as you sell a sheep." Again Leif's mother laughed. "Gunner loved her though, but not enough to change his habits, and she . . . she found somebody else after a while."

Leif looked surprised. "What do you mean?"

"You are already fifteen and should no longer be a child." Greta Helgasdaughter gave her son a sarcastic glance. "But then I don't think you are, or you wouldn't be running to Brattahlid so often."

"Whom did she find?" Leif stammered, blushing more out of anger than shame.

"Olaf! Saint Olaf!" Greta said mockingly, for she, too, had loved her cousin Olaf, and he had hurt her.

Suddenly the boy remembered the way Olaf Ulfson looked at his niece: longingly, as a dog looks at its master. "Is he," he asked, "her father?"

"She swore on her deathbed that Ingeborg was Gunner's." Leif's mother shrugged her shoulders. "Does it matter?" she asked and then answered her own question. "Nothing matters anymore, for we shall die here." Monotonously, as if she were reciting a lament, Greta Helgasdaughter pronounced each word with care. "We shall be the last Norsemen in Greenland and there will be no one left to bury us or put stones on our graves. The little people from the north will come and steal what is left of our things and our halls will be swallowed up by the earth."

"Maybe the king of Norway's boat will come," Leif said eagerly to comfort his mother.

"The ship may come in time for you." Greta placed her hand on her son's shoulder and for the first time Leif saw tears in her eyes. "But for me, and for Gunner too, though he does not know it, it is too late . . . Greenland is so terribly big; beyond the mountains stretches the ice, farther even than an eagle can see, however high it flies. Yet this place is not large enough for our dreams anymore."

Leif reached out to touch his mother, but she pushed him away and then, in her usual scolding tone, told him to stop bothering her.

When Leif joined his two friends he was no longer so eager to show them the spear, but they did go to their "hall." He felt very grown up with his new knowledge, which he could not share with anyone. It occurred to him that grownups must be filled with secrets such as he had heard, secrets they would carry to their graves.

As Leif had expected, Bjarne appreciated the spear.

Even Odd was impressed, though he did say that a handful of good iron fishhooks would have been of more use.

When Leif lay down to sleep that night he thought of Ingeborg. He wondered how much she knew of what his mother had told him. Gudrin, her mother, had died when she was only two years old. Suddenly he realized that no one had ever told him what she died from, and he felt certain that he knew. Gudrin Sigridsdaughter had taken her own life, that was another secret. In a flood of pity he thought, just as he closed his eyes in sleep, Ingeborg must never be told that, she must never know it.

5

Egil

SOME PEOPLE are like the inland ice that covers most of Greenland, they are filled with deep clefts and secret caves. And just as that eternal ice is perilous and treacherous to those who dare travel across it, so are these people dangerous to anyone rash enough to trust them.

Brought up on a small farm on the innermost part of Eriksfjord by a mother who cursed the weak-willed man she had married and a father ill fitted for the lonely life among the snow-covered mountains, Egil Sigurdson had learned early that the world of man was not much kinder than the nature that surrounded him. As the seal in winter needs to keep breathing holes open in the ice that covers the fjord, so Egil had certain dreams and ambitions that sustained him in his loneliness. He, like Leif, had guessed the hopelessness of the Norsemen's position in Greenland. On their secluded farm the boy had watched his parents' little flock of sheep grow smaller each year. When his mother died it had been he, rather than his father, who insisted that they move to Brattahlid.

Several times the boy had visited the farm built by Erik the Red, and though it was but a wreck of its former glory, in all of Egil's dreams he was its master.

There were already two other families living at Brattahlid and both had children the same age as Egil. Otkel Gode and his wife, Jodis, had three sons, Kolben, Teit, and Asgrim. Kolben was the oldest, but his seventeen years had taught him little. His younger brother Teit often called him stupid, but never to his face for Kolben was strong and easily offended.

The Gode brothers were proud of their ancestry and of their name, which came from some great-great-grandfather of theirs who had been the keeper of the temple to the gods at Bredefjord in Iceland. But that had been in heathen times, and their father, Otkel, was now of little importance, except in his own opinion.

Egil had a sharp eye for others' faults and imperfections. He never made a mistake about their vulnerability, it was their virtues and their strengths he would overlook. Kolben was the first person he befriended. The poor boy had never before been asked his opinion about anything, and Egil would not only ask, but listen as well to his answers. Teit was a proud boy who had suffered because his father was dependent upon Gunner Ulfson, who treated him as if he were a servant. Egil flattered him until, like a tame bird, he would eat out of his hand. Asgrim, the cleverest of the three, was also the youngest; he was won over by "secrets" that Egil shared with him and which he was "not to tell a soul."

Not until the Gode brothers acknowledged him as their leader did Egil pay attention to the other family at Brattahlid. Thorkil and Astrid were Gunner's servants and they had three children, Skule, Atle, and Gunhild. Thorkil, brought up by Gunner Ulfson's father, lacked the imagination ever to consider that servitude need not have been his fate. His wife, Astrid, was not stupid, but slovenly and greedy. She neither cared for nor disliked the intruder from the wilderness of the innermost part of Eriksfjord. The only person she showed any loyalty to, or love for, was Ingeborg, Gunner Ulfson's daughter.

Skule and his sister, Gunhild, joined Egil's hird without even knowing it. They were the kind who drifted with the current, it would not have entered their minds that they could have swum against it.

Their brother Atle was different. He was the oldest of the three, sixteen winters had gone by since he was born, and those years had chipped and formed him. He was a boy capable of learning from any master, but slow to acknowledge anyone as his superior. Egil did not trust him, but he respected him and listened to his opinions carefully.

In little more than a month Egil managed to become the master of his new home. Only three of the inhabitants remained unvanquished: Olaf, Ingeborg, and Egil's own sister, Bera. She was a curious little creature, Egil claimed — half human and half troll. Small she was, with hardly any neck to connect her little head to her body. The color of her eyes, was it gray or green? No one really knew, any more than anyone could guess her age correctly. Most thought her eleven or twelve years old, but in fact she was older than Egil. Born on Christmas Eve, the holiest night of the year, seventeen winters ago, she could lay claim to be treated as a woman. But because of her size she seldom was and, strangely enough, did not seem to mind.

As soon as she came to Brattahlid Bera had, as a matter of course, attached herself to Ingeborg. Egil used to refer to her sneeringly as Ingeborg's thrall. This was unfair, for Bera was no one's slave, as her brother knew well enough. At times Egil wondered whether his sister hated him. The thought made him uneasy, and he would dismiss it with a shrug or a "What do I care?" that was not convincing.

Ingeborg had accepted Bera as if their meeting was fated to happen. As soon as Leif left her, that spring afternoon when they watched the approach of the newcomers, Ingeborg hurried to greet them. To Sigurd and Egil she only nodded, but Bera she took by the hand. She had shown her her goats and all her treasures, and from the first night the girls shared a bed in the hall. Although Bera knew all of Ingeborg's secrets, Ingeborg did not know any of Bera's. This did not bother Ingeborg, because she did not even notice it. In spite of all their poverty, she was still a chieftain's daughter, brought up to be the center of the great house, the lone star burning in that eternal cold winter night which life in Greenland had become for the Norsemen.

Two weeks after the Ivarsons' arrival in Brattahlid Bera asked Ingeborg, during one of their long walks together, if she liked her brother, Egil. The girl thought long before she answered, not because she did not know her own opinion, but because she debated whether she should speak her mind.

Finally she said, looking away from her companion, "No, I don't like your brother."

"Neither do I." Bera smiled and then added, "And Egil doesn't like me either."

Ingeborg was more surprised than shocked, not so much by Bera's reply as by the casual manner in which it had been said. "Did you ever like him?" she asked.

"I don't know." Bera wrinkled her brow. "I was so young then myself, I mean, when he was small." She laughed. "It is funny to think that once we were all small babies."

The two girls were walking along the shore. When they came to the point where the cliffs rose steeply and the beach disappeared they sat down upon the grassy brink.

"Oh, I don't mind having been small, having been a child." While she spoke Ingeborg glanced down at herself, as if judging whether she might be a child still. "I am more frightened of what is to come."

"You mean getting married?" Bera grinned. "No one will marry me."

"Why shouldn't someone marry you?" Ingeborg's voice was not reassuring.

"Because of the way I look." Bera let herself fall backward into the grass and lay there for a moment looking up into the sky. "Egil says he is going to marry you," she declared, closing her eyes as if she were going to sleep.

"No, he won't!" Ingeborg shouted with fury.

"Egil always gets what he wants," Bera said, as if that was the end of the discussion.

"I will kill him before I marry him," Ingeborg exclaimed.

"You will have to." Bera sat up and nodded for emphasis as she repeated her words. "You will have to."

6

The First Encounter

SOONER OR later Leif and Egil were bound to meet, and as it happened a broken rake was the cause of their first encounter. That summer had been the warmest and driest that Leif could remember. So much hay was harvested that for once there was hope that all his father's sheep and goats would survive the winter. In many a past spring, by the time the snow had finally melted, the animals were so starved they had not had the strength to stand up. But this year Leif had cut grass in meadows where there had not been haymaking since the time when the Norsemen had had both cows and horses on Greenland.

Some of these pastures were merely little hollows offering just that bit of protection from the winds that was necessary for the grass to reach a height for cutting. In the spring Leif had repaired their three wooden rakes, whittling new teeth himself. One day Sven, his father's servant, returned from work with the broken handle of one of the rakes.

Leif was furious. There were no trees at Isafjord except dwarf birch and a willow that crawled humbly along the ground. They would furnish at best only teeth for a rake.

Across Eriksfjord from Brattahlid, beyond the stony plains near the shore, there was a valley where trees grew to a height of ten or even fifteen feet. It had long been Leif's wish to visit this place and bring back what wood he and his companions could carry. Now the broken rake gave him a good reason for doing so before winter. He also had hopes of finding some trees with branches shaped in such a manner that one could make a pitchfork out of them. They had once had one on the farm, but it had disappeared years ago.

It would have been by far the easiest to borrow Gunner Ulfson's boat and sail across Eriksfjord, but Leif knew that his uncle would either refuse or ask for half the timber as the price of his favor. Instead, they would have to walk all the way to the bottom of Eriksfjord and then almost as far on the other shore; the journey there and back would take about a week.

Besides Bjarne and Odd, the sons of Sven, two boys from a neighboring farm to the south of Magnus Eriksen's, who belonged to Leif's hird, were willing to go on the trip. Their names were Flose and Ulv. Their father, Rage, was a silent man whom God in his wisdom had given a wife who talked enough for two. Her name was Groa, and she could not keep quiet even in her sleep. Ulv, who was fourteen, was as talkative as his mother and Flose, who was fifteen, as tongue-tied as his father.

There was one farm on Isafjord that had not been abandoned, where a woman lived alone with her daughter. It was said of her that she knew more than the Lord's Prayer, her name was Unn the Wise. Her daughter, Katla, was seventeen and stronger than most of the men in Greenland, but as simple and harmless as a child of five. Tall and straight-limbed, she might have been beautiful had it not been for the expression on her face. It was as if she lacked a soul, and often she would sit open-mouthed staring at nothing at all. Her mother, Unn, sometimes became so angry at the sight of her daughter that she drove her with blows from their hut. Then the poor girl would come with tear-stained cheeks to Magnus Eriksen's hall. From the moment she first saw him, only a few days after he was born, Katla had loved Leif. He was always kind to her, though often her doglike devotion irritated him. Katla was pleased when Leif asked her if she would come with them to the valley of the glacier. Unn said that Leif only wanted her along because she could carry as much wood as the rest of them together, but Katla could not understand why there was anything wrong in that.

The day they set out was perfectly still; not the smallest puff of wind disturbed the water of the fjord, which formed a perfect mirror, doubling every iceberg floating on its blue surface. Leif walked in front, spear in hand, behind him came Bjarne, Odd, Flose, Ulv, and last of all Katla. The girl carried the heaviest burden, a large skin bag, besides Leif's blanket and her own. Bjarne had the only iron axe in Isafjord stuck in his belt; his blanket he carried rolled over his shoulder.

Odd held a strange, harpoonlike weapon in his hand — a wooden shaft four feet long with, tied at one end, two curved, jagged pieces of bone that almost met. The boy used it for fishing. He was very skillful with it, and many a fat trout had ended its life struggling between those two bone "jaws."

Leif had hoped to see Ingeborg as they passed not far from Brattahlid, but he was disappointed. On the strand where Gunner Ulfson's boat was beached a group of boys were sitting around a fire. Leif recognized most of them, but the tallest of the boys had his back to them. For a moment his feeling of his own importance and his natural curiosity fought a battle. At last curiosity won and Leif started down to the beach.

"It is Egil, Sigurd Ivarson's boy," Odd whispered to Leif, who nodded impatiently. When they were within a spear's length of each other Leif stood still and wished the other boy a good morning. Egil turned, grinned, and asked them their errand, but did not offer his hand. As the two groups faced each other each boy silently attempted to judge the strength and capability of his nearest rival. For somehow it was immediately clear to them all that they belonged to two camps confronting each other for the first, but not the last, time. A feeling of exultation swept through the children, as if the discovery of an enemy was a good reason for celebration. Leif's voice quavered as he explained where they were going, while through his mind the question of whether he was older than Egil kept bouncing around like a ball.

"You have far to go!" Mockingly, Egil looked at the boat drawn up on the beach, as if to say, We could sail you across the fjord if we wanted to.

"Aye, and therefore it is best we do not waste the morning." As Leif spoke he could not help glancing at the opposite shore, so near and yet so far away.

"Guests are always welcome at Brattahlid, but we do not hold on to them when they wish to leave." Smiling sarcastically, Egil held out his hand.

For a moment Leif thought of not taking it, but then he decided that that would be foolish.

"I could break his neck," Bjarne declared as soon as they were out of earshot.

"Did you feel the spear moving in your hand?" Odd asked.

"It wiggled like a worm." Leif laughed, for it had occurred to him, for one fleeting moment while Egil taunted him, that he could lift his spear and kill him. "It knew its target," he said and held the weapon high in the air.

"I think," Odd remarked, "that we might need other shafts than those used for rakes."

"Each of us shall make himself a spear," Leif ordered. "The points we can make out of sharpened bones."

Once more they all felt that strange feeling of exultation, and they lifted their feet high like little horses held within tight reins that wished to gallop.

7.

The Abandoned Farms

T HE JUBILATION that the youngsters had felt as they faced Egil and his hird soon disappeared and was followed by its very opposite. The first to feel this dejection, and the one who experienced it most deeply, was Leif. In his dreams he had seen himself as the savior of the Norsemen of Greenland, but not as a warrior. The thought of having to fight Egil when there was all of nature to battle against seemed stupid and wasteful. Yet, thinking back upon his meeting with the other boy, he could not visualize Egil and himself as friends. But need we be enemies? he asked with such fervor that he almost spoke out loud. Yes, if you want to be the leader, he answered himself, and smiled bitterly.

By the time the boys came to the first of the abandoned farms in the inner part of the fjord, Leif had decided that he would give up his claim to leadership if that sacrifice were necessary for their survival. It was a heroic decision and Leif enjoyed his unselfishness so much that his good humor returned. The fact that this loss did not have to take place in the foreseeable future, and that in the meantime he could arm his little army, contributed much to his regaining his spirit.

They sat down and rested by the ruin of the farmhouse. It had been abandoned so long that none of the youngsters could recall ever having heard of anyone living there. It was built on a headland from which you could see all the way to the bottom of Eriksfjord. The house was tiny, fourteen feet by eight, but built very solidly of stones that had been selected with care. Those walls will still be standing when each of us has long been dead, Leif thought dismally.

"He was so ugly." Katla's voice broke Leif's melancholy thoughts and he asked, a little surprised, "Who?"

"That boy." Katla sniffed, a habit she had even when her nose was not running, which was seldom.

"She means Egil." Odd laughed, while his brother, Bjarne, exclaimed, "He is a coward, I know."

Leif smiled and shook his head, for he felt sure that Egil was neither ugly nor faint-hearted. But it was typical of Katla to use beauty and ugliness, and Bjarne courage and cowardice, as the ultimates in virtue and wickedness.

"I thought him rather handsome," Odd said teasingly, but Katla knew the boy too well to defend her point of view. Odd had more success with his brother when, nodding in the direction of the innermost part of Eriksfjord, he said, "It must have been lonely in there. They say it is ghost-ridden too, that old mother Hildegun walks there in the night. It seems a bad place for a coward to choose to live."

"Aye, and that is why he left," Bjarne said with a scowl. "He was afraid like his father, they are both cowards."

Leif wanted to say something kind and appreciative to Bjarne and Katla, at the same time expressing his own very different opinion of Egil. "I think Odd is right, he is not a coward." While he spoke Leif looked at Bjarne. "At least not the ordinary kind who fears to leave the hall once the sun has set. Yet you may be right that he lacks the final kind of daring, that boldness which can face not death but life." Leif paused, surprised by his words and far from sure of what they really meant. Bjarne nodded with a self-satisfied expression on his face, as if Leif had stated his own opinion. Katla sniffed deeply and said, "But he is ugly." This made all the children laugh.

When they came to the innermost part of the fjord, they explored the farm that had belonged to Sigurd Ivarson. Although abandoned for only a month, the buildings already looked like ruins because the wood construction of the roofs had been removed and taken to Brattahlid. Situated beside a small river not far from a beach, it must have seemed a pleasant place to the man who first settled there. Flose, who seldom opened his mouth between meals, gave the opinion that the place was haunted, saying that he could feel an evil spirit. This made Bjarne, who was a very courageous boy except for his fear of ghosts, suggest that they walk on and camp for the night beyond the next river. Ulv declared that all of Greenland was haunted and that there were by now more ghosts than live people around. However, this opinion was rendered in so cheerful a voice that it made little impression on the others.

They had not walked far before they came to yet another abandoned farm. It too was a ruin and Leif thought that it might have been more than a hundred years since a fire had been lit on its hearthstone. Odd and Ulv declared that this was the very hut that old mother Hildegun had inhabited, and they suggested staying the night to see if she would not come around at midnight and "throw bones" to read their future. Bjarne was fool enough to declare that he would not stay for all of Gunner Ulfson's silver. Odd suggested that he could borrow Leif's spear, which to his delight made the boy shake his head and affirm very seriously, "Those ghosts are already dead, as all men know, and they cannot be killed again with sword or any other weapon unless it had been their own."

Ulv held his hand in front of his face to hide a smile, saying that he did not think old mother Hildegun had even owned a sword. Odd then suggested that they search the ruins for a wooden spoon that they could give to Bjarne, for if the old lady should come to visit them he could use it as a weapon to defend himself.

At last poor Bjarne understood that his brother and Ulv were making a fool of him. For a moment he thought of taking revenge in the only manner he knew and Odd, who could run faster than he and had felt his brother's fist before, was ready to make his escape, but then Bjarne merely walked on, ignoring them.

Leif called Odd and he came smiling, falling in step by his side as if nothing had happened. "You are hard on your poor brother," Leif said. As Odd did not disagree but merely laughed, he added, "I wish you wouldn't be."

"If he should beat me, would you stop him?" Odd asked.

"Not if it were an honest fight," Leif answered. "And if he did you no harm."

"There is no such thing as an honest fight, one is always stronger than the other." Odd looked away for a moment. "If Egil and his friends had attacked us, would that have been an honest fight?"

"I think there were more of them than we were." Leif wrinkled his brow, trying to remember.

"It does not matter." Odd laughed. "My brother wins every time with his fists, so I take my revenge with words. But I shall let him be until we get home."

"I will thank you for that." Leif smiled. "For on a hike like this it is best we all stay friends."

It was getting late, the sun had long set, but it was still summer and the sky was so light that only a few stars were visible. Leif walked a little ahead of the rest, searching for a place to camp for the night. Suddenly, silhouetted against the night sky, he saw yet another small house, this one not in ruins. His heart leaped at the thought of a warm fire though he could see no smoke emerging from the roof. He ran the last bit of the way, but as he got nearer he saw to his disappointment that here, too, the roof was not intact, but had a gaping hole.

Somehow he knew, as he reached out for the hasp of the door, that whatever was beyond that frail wooden barrier would bring no comfort. The lower leather hinge had broken and he had to lift the door in order to open it. As he did so, the upper hinge broke as well, and the door fell crashing to the ground. Leif stood in the doorway contemplating the little room, which contained only a table, two stools, and a plank bed. In the misty silver night of a northern summer, beneath the skins that had served as blankets, he could dimly see the outline of the bodies of those who had last called this lonely hut their home. Lifting the skins with two fingers, he drew them back far enough to uncover their faces. The woman's hair was long and gray, the man's white and spare. They had been dead a long time and by now the bones seemed ready to break through the skin. Leif shivered as he let their bedding fall back and cover them once more.

Odd and Ulv were the first to catch up with him. Odd looked at him questioningly.

"Go and see for yourself." Leif shook his head. "Not that it is a pleasant sight."

When Odd returned he whispered to Leif, "Don't let Bjarne see it."

8

The Valley of the Trees

"Dᴵᴰ ʏᴏᴜ know who they were?" Odd asked Leif, as he bent down to blow life into the little fire he had miraculously ignited.

"No." Leif shook his head. "My father or my uncle Ravn will know. It must have been awful to die like that, all alone."

"You think so?" Odd looked up from what he was doing.

"Don't you?" Leif asked, surprised.

"I am not sure, I like being alone. When a dog is sick it hides, and if it dies, it dies alone." The pieces of kindling burst into flames. Odd took the strange little bow and the stick he had used to make the fire and put them away by his blanket.

"Who taught you to make a fire?" Leif asked.

"In the country north of the moon, where the white bear is king, I learned the art," Odd replied laughing, but noticing the expression on Leif's face, he added good-humoredly, "The little people taught it to me, and gave me the firebow."

Leif looked around to make sure that none of the other boys was within earshot, then he asked, "What are they like?"

"Different from us." Odd placed a larger piece of wood on the fire and acted as if he had answered the question.

"Different from you or from me?" Leif forced himself to smile.

"Different from you and from me, too." Odd moved a little away from the fire, seating himself on a boulder.

"In what way?" Leif asked eagerly, for he had only seen the little people once in his life and that at some distance.

"They have never lived anywhere else." Odd threw a pebble into the air and caught it again.

"Neither have I, nor you." Leif could not hide his growing annoyance at the way Odd answered his questions.

"Haven't we?" Odd grinned. "I think that half the time, at least in our dreams, we live in Norway." The boy laughed. "Sometimes I think our souls fly at night like birds through the darkness to that country which not even our grandfathers have seen. The little people don't, in their dreams they catch fat seals or a white bear."

"And you, do you dream of Norway too?" Leif's voice was soft now, for not only had all his anger left him, but he felt too that in Odd he might find a friend who would understand him.

"No, I don't." Odd threw the pebble away and then picked up another small stone. "But neither do I dream of catching fat seals."

"But that is what you want?" Leif asked.

"Maybe." Odd let the new-found stone drop from his hand as he turned a little to look Leif straight in the face. "If I dreamt myself to Norway, what would I be there that would be greater than what I am here — a hewer of wood and drawer of water? If I dreamt myself an earl I would only dream myself a fool."

"There is not much wood to cut in Greenland." Leif laughed, for the bitterness of the other boy and the truth of what he had said embarrassed him. "I do not want to dream of Norway," he added.

"I will go to the river and see if I can spear some trout." Odd rose and grasped his weapon. As he left he smiled and said to Leif, "But you don't want to dream of fat seals either."

Leif was about to answer but Odd gave him no chance to do so, he was gone.

Two days they had spent so far in the valley of the glacier, they had cut wood enough for spears and rakes.

Leif even found two tree trunks from which he cut a pair of pitchforks, one with three prongs and the other with two. They climbed the mountain that divided the glacier into three parts, one arm stretching down to a deep inlet of Eriksfjord. It was from this that the icebergs on the fjord were born. Another smaller arm emptied itself into a lake and the third came to a halt in the valley. The water from the melting ice formed a river that, by the time it reached the fjord, had become so deep and turbulent that it was difficult to cross. Halfway between the shore and the glacier the trees grew. Most of them were no more than six feet tall and their trunks no heavier than a man's wrist, but some reached more than double that length. From the fine branches of the birch, Katla had bound brooms and Flose a basket.

"On our journey back I want to bury the old people we found." Leif looked sharply at his followers, for he feared that they might revolt. The thought that the old Norse couple might lie unburied in their hut forever seemed somehow an affront to his own honor.

"If we don't, they might come at night and kill our sheep!" Bjarne's voice shook. "Ghosts often revenge themselves upon those who are alive. Did you look them in the eye?" The boy looked eagerly at Leif, half enjoying the thought of the horror that would descend upon his leader if he had.

"No, I didn't." Leif lied, for he was not sure whether or not he had, but felt it was safest to deny it. The sight of the corpses in the hut by the fjord had frightened him a great deal more than he cared to admit.

"That is well." Bjarne, who had not entered the hut himself, turned to his brother and asked if he had looked into the faces of the dead.

Odd had returned with two large trout that he had caught in the river and was roasting them on a spit. At first he acted as if he had not heard his brother. Pretending to be busy with his cooking, he answered only when Bjarne repeated the question, and then said in a tone of voice filled with contempt, "I did not know that you knew so much about ghosts, brother. But I suppose it should not surprise me, knowing how afraid you are of the dark." Flose and Ulv laughed, but Odd only scowled at them.

"I would not want anyone who might even be kinsmen of ours to be eaten by foxes." Leif felt a little ashamed that Bjarne had actually managed to frighten him too, for he had not really thought of the two old people haunting him as ghosts when he had said he wanted to see them buried.

"We can't bury them near their own house," Odd said, turning the fish as he spoke. "There was not earth enough to dig graves, though plenty of stones for a cairn."

"They chose a poor place to settle," Leif agreed.

"Maybe that was the only place they were allowed to have; the chieftains, like Erik the Red, took what was best and then gave their friends the picking of what was left. When they had finished the friendless could have whatever rock-filled valley the others overlooked. Those first served got too much, and those served last went hungry." With those words Odd placed the fish on two flat stones and drew out the sticks he had used as spits, bidding them all to eat.

"Since we are all served at the same time none of us, I hope, will go hungry," Leif said good-naturedly, wondering why Odd seemed so filled with hatred. Now more than ever he wanted the boy as his friend. He drew his knife and, handing it to Odd, asked him to divide the fish. When this was done Leif carefully took the piece he judged to be the smallest.

9

The Burial

THE BURIAL of the two old people brought Leif and Odd closer together. Bjarne had refused to enter the house and neither Flose nor Ulv had been eager to cross its threshold. Leif had ordered the boys to clear a piece of ground near the house and to set about collecting stones for a cairn. Then he asked Odd if he would help him. Odd, instead of giving an answer, opened the door to the hut. For a moment the two boys stood in silence, contemplating the bed, then Leif asked in a voice not altogether steady, "Is it true that if you look into a dead man's eyes his soul will take power over yours?"

"I think the dead are gone — where, I don't know — but I do not think they ever come back here to earth, and even if they did, I don't think they can harm us. Sometimes when I have been away all alone and slept beneath the stars, I have thought about it. For at night when you cannot see anything that is close to you the world grows larger and you yourself become so tiny." Odd stopped as if he was embarrassed at having talked so long, but then he continued, "I think the evil men do is buried with them, it is the living we need fear. Why should those two old people stay here once they are dead? And why should they care to scare poor Bjarne?" Odd smiled and shook his head.

Leif nodded eagerly in agreement, though he had no wish to look at the bodies of the old couple again. "They are lying on some skins; if we carry them carefully," he said, "we need not uncover them."

As the two boys took hold of the skins that had formed a part of the bedding, both of them silently prayed that it would not burst where the sheepskins had been sewn together. They were lucky and managed to carry their burden to the place Leif had chosen for the burial. But as they lowered it a hand and part of an arm appeared from beneath the skins. The boys looked with horror at it, for it almost seemed to beckon them. Leif glanced at Odd and then bent down and pushed the arm back underneath the covers. His first thought had been to do it with his foot, for he had no wish to touch the almost skeletonlike claw. But then, mostly because he feared Odd would think him a coward, he had done it with his hand.

In silence the children started to carry stones and to cover the bodies with them. When the first layer of stones had hidden the corpses from sight, Leif beckoned

Odd into the hut again. He wished to see if there was anything of value that they could use, but he did not want to search the place alone.

"I wonder if there is anything worth taking with us," Leif explained.

"I doubt it," Odd said, looking around. "They were very old and, having no young ones to help, I think they starved to death this spring. The ice on the fjord was slow in breaking."

"Still, they might have had a knife." Leif searched a corner of the room where an upright loom was standing. It had not been used for many years, and a few of the loom stones were still hanging from their threads. "Their sheep must have been dead, since they had no wool to weave with."

"Look." Odd had a leather purse in his hands, he held it out for Leif to see. "It is empty," he said.

"I would have been more surprised if it had been filled with silver." Leif smiled.

"So would I," said Odd, "but you don't throw your empty purse in the middle of the room. Someone has been here before us and has taken the few coins it contained. I doubt if you will find a knife or anything else of value."

"I think you are right." Leif leaned against the wall. "I actually thought so when we were here last, that hole in the roof looks not so much as if it was worn by the weather, but more as if it was made on purpose. Why did the old ones not go to Sigurd Ivarson or to Gunner Ulfson at Brattahlid?"

"Do you think they would have been welcomed in either place?" Odd asked mockingly.

"Neither by Sigurd nor by Gunner, but Olaf would have made them welcome."

"And who is chieftain at Brattahlid? Not Olaf Ulfson, he has to beg for his food from his brother himself."

"You are right." Leif nodded. "And you are right too that we shall find nothing here. The ravens, the scavengers, have been here before us."

As the two youngsters stood outside the hut and watched the others pile stones on the cairn, Odd said, "I hope the old ones were dead when they last had visitors."

Leif looked at the barren mountain behind them and then across the fjord. He could clearly make out Brattahlid. How doubly lonesome it must have been, he thought, to be able to see other human beings so near and yet so far away. "I hope so too," he said and then repeated the words, "I hope so too."

When the cairn was built Leif found two sticks and, tying them together, made a cross. He felt he should say something, repeat some kind of prayer, but he did not know any. "They have gone to God," he finally said and then, looking at Bjarne, he added, "and they will not come back here."

The big, strong boy nodded thoughtfully and then muttered, more to himself than to anyone else, "It is true I think, they will not come back, but there are others who won't lie still in their graves."

"And who might they be?" asked Odd.

"It is well known," the boy pleaded, "that Gunner Ulfson's wife, Gudrin Sigridsdaughter, has been seen." Bjarne tried to catch the eye of Flose or Ulv for encouragement.

"We put stones on the dead so they won't come and haunt us, don't we?" Katla suddenly said daringly, though she was not courageous enough to look at Leif while she said it.

"I did it so that the foxes would not make a meal of them," Leif protested. Then, realizing that there was no point in continuing the argument, he gave orders that they should push on homeward.

As they walked carrying their burdens Odd came up beside Leif. "You know," he said, "that the little people believe that even the animals have spirits that live after they have been killed."

"Do you believe that?" Leif asked.

"I don't know." Odd glanced back, one could still see the cairn. "But why should the dead wish men any harm? The spirit of a dead seal must remember all the fish it has eaten itself," he said with a laugh as he fell back and let Leif walk on alone.

Since the wood they had gathered was hardly more than sticks, their load was not so much heavy as uncomfortable to carry. They rested often, and once they made a regular camp and lit a fire. Leif recalled that the summer before Odd had been away during the late haymaking season and everyone had thought him dead, even his father and mother. He must have spent that time with the little people, he thought, for when he had returned he would not tell where he had been. The night they camped Leif asked Odd if he spoke the language of the little people. The boy shrugged his shoulders in his usual manner when asked a question he did not want to answer. But Leif pressed him until he finally admitted that he knew some words in their language.

"Will you leave us and go to them?" Leif asked. Odd shrugged his shoulders again as if to say, "I don't know," but then he thought better of it and replied, "I do not know what I am going to do." They were sitting near their little fire, which Odd kept alive with tiny pieces of wood. "What will I do if I stay at Isafjord?" he finally asked.

"We are so few left" — Leif looked thoughtfully into the flames — "that it does not matter who your parents are and whether you can claim kinship with all the earls of Norway."

"I know that sometime far back, longer than any of us can recall, someone brought a thrall to Greenland who is my ancestor. I lay no claim to kinship with any earls." Odd was silent for a moment, then with a crooked smile he said, "The little people have never heard of earls or thralls."

If he was rebuffed by Odd each time he tried to make him his friend, this did not make Odd's friendship less desirable, less valuable in Leif's eyes. He wanted someone who could and would understand his dreams, his ambitions, and whom at the same time he could respect. Odd was the only boy he knew of who fulfilled this wish.

The children did not come close to Brattahlid on their return journey, they had no wish to meet Egil and his hird while carrying their loads of timber. Still, Egil or some of his friends must have seen them, for they were clearly visible from the farm as they trudged up toward the pass to Isafjord. Their spirits were high when they saw the familiar sight of their fjord. Home is never so pleasant, so desirable, as when you return from a long journey. Leif looked forward to showing his pitchforks to his father.

But little notice was taken of them or of the wood they brought with them when they were told the news.

"They came" — Magnus Eriksen became angrier as he told the story — "a whole horde of them, and took one of our haystacks, made it up into bundles, and carried it to Brattahlid. If I had had a sword — but I have none, it was given to Ravn and he would not use it. Maybe he was right, they were too many and we were too old." Magnus Eriksen paused for a moment and then said in wonder, "But they were no more than children!"

"It is Egil," Leif exclaimed. "It is he who put them up to it."

"Good that we have shafts for spears," Ulv said. But Odd merely looked troubled.

10

The Sword

WHEN HE was told of Egil's raid upon his father's farm, Leif's first thought was to arm his hird and pay a visit to Brattahlid. First thoughts, though, are often foolish thoughts, and as soon as he realized that the hay that had been stolen was of a second cutting and would in no way endanger his father's sheep, even if the winter came early and lasted long, he had wiser thoughts. Still, the following day the children were busy making spears so they would at least be able to defend themselves should Egil raid them again.

Magnus Eriksen had great difficulty getting over what had happened. The fact that he had been attacked by what he called children had upset him. He declared to anyone who would listen that he would not have been more surprised had the sun ceased to rise in the morning or had the moon fallen from the sky. Leif's mother's voice grew even sharper, and the hall was not a pleasant place to be. She blamed what had happened on the ingratitude of children in general, making Egil and his hird the proof of it. But since Egil was not there to scold she let her bad temper loose on Leif.

A few days after he came home Leif went to visit his uncle Ravn, not only to hear from his mouth what had happened, but to seek his advice as well. He planned to visit Brattahlid alone and unarmed, or with Odd if he was willing. He would act as if what had happened was not important, and make a gift to them of the hay that had been stolen. He still hoped to make Egil understand that there were matters more important than themselves at stake in Greenland.

"I doubt if you will make the boy see straight," his uncle said as soon as Leif explained his plan. "He was born with a worm in his eye, I have known that kind. My advice to you is, don't trust him ever."

"But it is so foolish," Leif argued. "Here we are not enough Norsemen to farm the land and he turns robber. I do not understand it, for he is not a fool." Leif paused. "If he had told me that they were in need of hay at Brattahlid, I would have given it to them."

Ravn Eriksen shook his head. "By all means do talk to Gunner Ulfson, but don't trust him. See if you can get his brother, Olaf, alone; he is a fool but he might be able to tell you something. Best of all, talk to Ingeborg if they will let you. She is kind like her uncle Olaf but, unlike him, she is not a fool."

"Why should I not be able to talk to Ingeborg?" This

possibility had never occurred to Leif. "Who would keep me from seeing her?"

"I don't know." Ravn Eriksen lowered his voice as if he were telling a secret. "But I do know that Egil and the other boys must have come here with Gunner Ulfson's knowledge, if not his permission. That means things have changed at Brattahlid since you were last there. I have known Egil's father and mother. His father was a sparrow, but if he takes after his mother then he, not Gunner, will soon be sitting in the chieftain's seat at Brattahlid."

"I will go tomorrow." Leif rose. "If there have been changes at Brattahlid we should know of them."

Ravn Eriksen told the boy to wait and then, from the same corner of the room where he had brought forth the spear, he took a sword and handed it to his nephew. "I was not going to give it to you yet, but now you may have need of it."

Leif held the sword in his hands. It was roughly made and in Norway it would not have been thought a great weapon, but Leif had only seen one other sword in his life. That had belonged to Gunner Ulfson and had not been finer. Every bit of his boy's heart wanted it, yet he handed it back to his uncle, saying, "If Egil is chieftain of Brattahlid and I cannot pluck that worm from his eye which keeps him from seeing, then I shall call for it again."

As Ravn Eriksen put the sword back, he mumbled as if to himself, "I would go with you if I were any help, but Gunner and I care as little for each other as the herring does for the shark."

Then, speaking a little louder, he wished Leif luck. As the boy left the room one single tear ran down the cheek of the older man, who smiled bitterly as he wiped it away.

As soon as Leif left his uncle's hall, he went looking for Odd. He wanted the boy to go with him to Brattahlid for he felt that he was the only one in his hird who would be a help. It was not so much strength as cleverness and good judgment he would be in need of. But Odd was nowhere to be found; neither his mother nor his father had seen him since morning. Leif finally found Bjarne down by the bay, and he said that his brother had left very early and had taken his blanket, his spear for catching fish, and some other things, which meant that he would not come back soon. "He's gone to his friends the little people," the boy said with contempt. "I would not go with him," he added for good measure.

"Where do they have their hall?" Leif asked. He felt fairly certain that Odd had not asked his brother to accompany him.

"Hall?" Bjarne laughed. "They live in tents and smell of whale oil."

"They can't do that in the winter," Leif objected.

"Winter or summer they always smell of whale oil," Bjarne said sourly.

"I mean they can't live in tents in the winter." Leif smiled, Bjarne was obviously jealous of his brother's friendship with the little people.

"They go somewhere else when winter comes, farther out toward the sea where they are nearer the open water. The ice in our part of the fjord grows too thick for them to fish and for the seals they hunt to make their breathing holes. They don't have any sheep." The last sentence was said as if the keeping of sheep made someone a vastly superior being.

"How far away are their tents?" Leif asked.

"Over there, not far from here." Bjarne nodded in the general direction of where the little people could be found.

Leif was disappointed that he would have to go to Brattahlid alone. "Have you been there?"

"No, but one of them came here." Bjarne laughed. "He was older than me, but though he had lived more summers, he was small like this." Bjarne held out his hand to show his height. "If you tied one of my hands behind my back, I could still have beaten him," he said happily.

Leif nodded, thinking what a fool Bjarne was to think that strength was everything.

The only weapon Leif carried as he set out for Brattahlid was his knife. He had thought of taking the spear but in the end decided that would be unwise. It might endanger rather than protect him, for it might serve as an excuse for attacking him.

It was a beautiful day, the sky was clear but there was a taste of fall in the wind. Leif set out early, wanting to be home before sunset, for already the nights were cold. When he came to the pass from which he could see down to Brattahlid and Eriksfjord, he stopped and sat down, as was his habit. He was fond of that particular place. From up here, listening to the little waterfall nearby, he could dream, with all that part of Greenland that he loved and knew best stretched out in front of him.

Two eagles were flying high above Brattahlid. All of a sudden one swooped down on the other as if to attack it. Leif had never before seen two eagles fight so late in the year; the mating season was long over. He smiled, for he could not help thinking what kind of omen Gunner Ulfson would have seen in that.

Just as he was ready to get up he heard a noise down in the crag in the cliff where the waterfall was. He jumped to his feet, his hand on his knife.

"Are you Leif?" a voice asked. He stared in wonder at the little creature who was looking up at him. She was the size of an eight- or nine-year-old child but did not look like one. For a moment Leif thought that she belonged to the little people, but her features were more like a Norsewoman's. "I am Bera," she said as she made her way up the steep side of the crack in the mountain,

"Sigurd Ivarson's daughter, and I have been sent by Ingeborg Gudrinsdaughter to seek you out."

"How did you know I would be here?" Leif smiled at her as he sat down again, to make their sizes more equal.

"When we saw you returning carrying your loads of wood, Ingeborg said, 'Leif will come.' I have been here every day since then." Bera smiled.

"And what message do you bring me from Ingeborg?" Leif asked the girl, who was now standing in front of him. "I am sorry that I did not come sooner," he added.

"That does not matter, I did not mind waiting here." Bera looked at Leif and then said, "Ingeborg said I should know you because you were so handsome."

Leif laughed. "And now that you have seen me, do you find me so?" he asked.

"Yes, you are handsome." The girl sat down upon the ground, tucking her legs under her, which made her seem even smaller than she was. "Ingeborg is very beautiful, is she not?" she asked.

"Yes." Leif wrinkled his brow, for he had not really thought about it nor, for that matter, about whether he was handsome or not. He and Ingeborg had known each other since they were tiny children, but now as he conjured her picture he realized that she was beautiful. "Is that what she sent you up here for, to tell me I am handsome and to ask me if I think that she is beautiful?" he asked teasingly.

"No, that is not the reason." Bera shook her head very seriously. "I just wanted to know."

"And now you do." Leif grinned. "But what message do you carry from Ingeborg?"

"She asks you not to come to Brattahlid." Bera plucked a straw of grass and put it in her mouth. "She is afraid that Egil will kill you."

"And do you also think that Egil will kill me?" Leif asked.

"He will try." Bera looked up at Leif and smiled as if she had said something pleasant.

"But why should he want to kill me?" the boy asked, though somewhere in the back of his mind he knew not only that the girl was right, but also why Egil hated him.

"Just because . . ." Bera paused, searching for the right words, but as she could not find them she repeated what she had said. "Just because."

"That is not much of a reason." Leif laughed.

"Day and night cannot be at the same time. You are what you are and he is what he is." Bera had taken the straw out of her mouth while she spoke. She was just about to put it back when instead she threw it away and said, "You are like two rams in a flock of sheep, who will fight until there is only one left."

"Or until the shepherd slaughters one of them."

"But there aren't any shepherds left in Greenland." Bera was about to pluck a new straw when Leif got up. "Have you any message for Ingeborg?" she asked.

"None that I cannot bring her myself." Leif looked down at the tiny girl at his feet. "You wait here until I am down by the hall. I do not think it would be wise for Egil, or anyone for that matter, to see us together." Bera held up her hand as if she were going to say something, but she didn't, and Leif with long strides walked down the path to Brattahlid.

11

A New Chieftain at Brattahlid

LEIF DID not speculate about what might await him at Brattahlid as he strode down the path to the farm. He thought about his cousin Ingeborg, for Bera's words had made an impression. He had never considered before whether she was beautiful or not. What you see every day you often do not notice. It is not so much that you underestimate it as that you have never made a judgment concerning its value or virtue. Ingeborg to Leif had been like the fjord and the mountains round his home. It was as if a stranger had suddenly come and told him that Isafjord was one of the most beautiful landscapes in the whole world. He would then have seen it with the stranger's eye, as if he had never seen it before. He had always taken for granted that he and Ingeborg would marry once they were grown up. So had everyone else, and they were jestingly referred to as "the little sweethearts."

Now, as he recalled their childhood, he suddenly saw Ingeborg as a person apart from himself. Bera had given him the "stranger's eye," and because of that he was eager to see Ingeborg again.

A few hundred yards from Brattahlid Leif met Atle. They had known each other since childhood and were nearly the same age. Although Atle's parents were servants of Gunner Ulfson, the boys had played together and Leif had always liked Atle. He greeted him in a friendly manner, asking for news as if nothing had happened.

"Everything is . . ." Atle paused, obviously embarrassed by the warmth of Leif's greeting, and then said, "as it should be."

"I have been away from Isafjord for some days, and while I was away we had visitors." Leif smiled. "Were you one of them?"

"Yes, Gunner Ulfson sent us for some hay that you owed him." Atle did not meet Leif's gaze. "I am sorry you were not there," he mumbled.

"It must have been some very old debt, for I knew nothing of it and neither did my father." Trying to catch Atle's eye but unable to do so, Leif asked, "How is my cousin Ingeborg?"

"Very well, I think," Atle stammered, his cheeks growing red.

"Her father and Olaf, they are well too?" Leif was aware that he was torturing the poor boy, who had only one wish — to escape.

"Oh, Leif!" The boy almost shouted his name. "Be careful, there are those now at Brattahlid who wish you nothing but harm."

No sooner had Atle said this than he turned and ran away. "I am not totally without friends here," Leif mumbled to himself, "having been warned twice."

Gunner Ulfson was sitting in the chieftain's seat at the end of the table in the hall when Leif entered. Egil was standing on one side of the chair, Teit Gode on the other, as if they were the two statues that decorated the seat in the olden times. They knew I was coming, Leif thought to himself as he hailed Gunner Ulfson, calling him "cousin" and "kin."

"Leif, son of Magnus Eriksen, you are welcome in our hall." Gunner spoke ceremoniously, as if the boy were an earl and he king. "How is my cousin Greta and how fares everyone at Isafjord?"

Leif almost smiled but, looking at Egil whose face was as immobile as if his features had been cut out of wood, he decided it would be wiser not to. "My mother is well, and sends her greetings to her cousin," he answered. Then, shifting his gaze from Gunner Ulfson to Egil, he said, "My father, too, greets you and bids me tell you that should you be in need of hay for your sheep you need not take what might be freely given."

"Gunner Ulfson took nothing that was not his." Egil spoke very slowly, as if he suspected Leif of being hard of hearing. "You at Isafjord, like everyone else in Green-

80

land, are under the protection of the chieftain of Brattahlid."

"I did not know we were in need of protection." Leif shifted his gaze and Gunner Ulfson moved uncomfortably in his seat.

"When Erik, the son of Thorvald who was the son of Asvald Ulfson, came to Greenland and settled here at Brattahlid he gave his kin and friends land to hold," Gunner Ulfson said falteringly.

"True," Leif interrupted, "and both you and my mother can claim kinship with Erik the Red, as he was called."

"He gave the land as a free gift, but to be held under his chieftainship," Gunner Ulfson argued.

"And now if he came back he could give most of it away again." Leif looked at Egil as he spoke. "Most of the halls of the Norsemen have sunken roofs, and no one walks the paths between the farms but a lone fox hunting for food. To the northwest there is not a single Norseman alive anymore, only here on Eriksfjord, at Gardar and Herjolfness are there still Norsemen left. Is this the time for us to fight each other?"

"We have no wish to fight you from Isafjord, or anyone else," Egil said, taking one step forward. "If you will accept him who rules Brattahlid as your chieftain and serve him, there will be no quarrel between us."

"If he rules well I think he will have no difficulty in finding those who will serve him out of friendship. But if the chieftain of Brattahlid believes us slaves and not freeborn he shall find that he is mistaken."

For a moment everyone in the hall was silent, then Gunner Ulfson asked Leif to sit down, calling him "cousin" in too friendly a manner for the boy's taste. Egil called Teit Gode to his side and whispered something in his ear, probably a command of some kind, for Teit left the hall.

"And did you get the wood you wanted in the valley of ice?" Egil asked as he sat down on the bench across from Leif.

"We did, for rakes, pitchforks, and for . . ." Leif paused and then added, "Spears."

"Spears are good for hunting seals, or if you should meet a white bear," Egil said as Leif grinned. "Or someone who is not your friend."

"In those stories told of the old times" — Leif kept his gaze on Egil while he spoke — "it was said that no man should ever be far from his weapons, even when working in the field. I thought that custom was not needed in Greenland, since sickness and hunger are our only enemies and against them no spear is sharp enough."

"True we have grown soft," Egil replied, "like the stone found here that we make into the bowls we drink from. Misfortune has carved us hollow like them." For a moment he looked up toward Gunner Ulfson and a contemptuous smile spread across his face. "But not all are like that, some are hard like the stones from the mountains."

"True, such stones cannot be carved. If you hit them they splinter," Leif said softly, as if what he said was of no importance. He glanced at Gunner Ulfson. The older man felt the youngster's gaze and looked away.

"Where is my cousin Olaf and where is Ingeborg?" Leif asked.

"My brother is not well," Gunner said, shrugging his shoulders.

"Is he in the church? If he is, I shall go and see him." When Leif stood up, Egil rose from his seat at the same moment as if he were his shadow. "Come and I will show you the church," he said.

Leif noticed, as Egil threw open the door, that the hinges had been mended. At first he could not see anything that had been changed, for the bit of light that penetrated the sheep's bladder covering the two small windows left the room in a perpetual gloom. But as his eyes accustomed themselves to it he saw that the large wooden cross that Olaf had fashioned in rough carpentry and hung behind the stone altar was gone, and so were the two bronze candlesticks. There was a strange smell, too. Leif walked forward to the stone altar, in front of which Olaf had prayed so often and so earnestly. It was covered by something sticky, he touched it, it was blood. For a moment, a feeling of horror swept over him as he thought that it was his cousin

Olaf's blood that had smeared his hand, but then he noticed some tufts of wool, and the relief was so great that he almost laughed. "What have you been doing here?" he asked. "Can you find no better place to slaughter your sheep?"

"This is no longer the home of Him who was called the White Christ but of Odin and Thor, and to them we have sacrificed a ram." Leif thought that Egil smiled but in the darkness it was hard to guess the expression on his face.

"It is many hundred years since Christ came to Greenland," Leif said, turning and walking toward the door. "The old gods are but names to frighten children."

"Who knows who rules the sun and moon and stars and men's lives? What has Christ done for us?" Egil spat out the last words as Leif passed him.

The light blinded Leif as he stepped outside. He did not immediately notice two boys standing nearby, Asgrim and Teit Gode, each of them carrying a spear.

"I have something to say to you," Egil told Leif as they stood in the doorway of the church. He smiled mockingly. "I hope you have washed your ears this morning, for it is of importance and I will not say it twice."

12

Bera

For a while Bera had watched Leif intently as he walked down the mountainside. Then with a sigh she climbed back down the gap in the mountain to the little waterfall. Downstream was a small pool of still water, and the girl leaned down on all fours to look into it. "You are not beautiful," she said aloud, staring at the girl who looked back at her. The features reflected in the clear water were not so much ugly as strange. Her eyes were farther apart than is usual and the nose, though perfectly formed, was very small. But the worst was that nature, repenting her parsimony in noses, had decided to be much more generous in giving a mouth to Bera's small face. She made a grimace and the girl in the water wrinkled up her face, at which Bera stuck out her tongue and then disturbed the water with her hand, destroying the image.

"No, I am not beautiful," she said again, and then lay

down on a grassy patch and looked up at the sky. He is handsome, she thought, and good, Ingeborg is right about that, but is he clever enough for my brother? Though she did not care for Egil, he was still her kin and for a moment she wanted him to be the cleverer of the two. But then because she knew the depth of his hate, she changed her mind.

Having been brought up in so lonely a place as the innermost part of Eriksfjord, Bera was used to talking and arguing with herself. She had invented playmates when small and they had been so real to her that she cried when she imagined that they had been hurt. Even now as a grownup — she would be eighteen before the year was out — she could keep up conversations with herself for hours.

It is natural that he hates him, for Egil is like night and Leif like the day and the two cannot be at the same time, she thought, watching a lone falcon in the sky. They are alike too — she smiled at the idea — for neither is afraid.

She leaned on her elbow to watch a snow sparrow chirruping nearby. Egil is like the falcon who will eat you without a thought, she noted with a grin, and made a noise that made the sparrow fly a few paces away. It landed again and looked at her with its little beady eyes.

"How do you like the name Bera?" she asked the sparrow, who warbled one short note in reply. "You are right, it is not a pretty name, but I don't care if it is ugly," she said as if she understood what the sparrow had said. Then she lay back again folding her hands beneath her head; the falcon was no longer to be seen, the sky was clear and cloudless.

"That is a lie, Bera!" The girl spoke so loudly, admonishing herself for having said something untrue, that the little snow sparrow flew away. "I do care, I want to be as beautiful as Ingeborg," she said and closed her eyes as if she were going to sleep.

Down in the hollow where she lay the sun was so warm that she dozed for a little while, then was awakened by the ever inquisitive sparrow coming back to investigate who had invaded its territory. It chirruped so loudly near her that the girl opened her eyes. As she noticed the little bird looking at her, its head askew, she burst out laughing. If Bera was not beautiful, her laughter was as sweet as the sound of the water falling on the stones nearby. She dipped her hands in the pool and washed her face, to get rid of her sleepiness more than any dirt. Then she stood up and climbed once more to the path that led to Brattahlid. She could no longer see Leif, or anyone for that matter, so she hurried down the path as fast as her short legs could carry her.

As there are no trees or bushes in Greenland it is difficult to hide; some big boulder might do for a while, but sooner or later you have to come into the open. Bera knew that anyone at Brattahlid who happened to glance up toward the mountain would probably see her, but she hoped that enough time had gone by that they would not connect her with Leif. She kept a sharp watch on the farm below and noticed that two boys — she could not see who they were — seemed to be standing guard by Olaf Ulfson's hut. She knew that Olaf, whom she thought a fool, loved his young cousin. He had baptized Leif and was his godfather too. She decided to find out exactly what the boys were doing, she suspected they were there to keep Leif from seeing his cousin. Olaf Ulfson had stayed in bed since Egil had taken his church from him; he lay there with his face to the wall, answering no one except Ingeborg. To her he spoke, but what he said was wild and strange, like a nightmare or the talk of one whom fever has robbed of his senses.

The two boys were Kolben and Skule, which was lucky for Bera, for Skule especially was frightened of her. He believed that she knew witchcraft, and she had merely to look at him to make him shake and shiver with fear.

"What are you two doing here?" she asked as she came up to them.

"We are guarding the house," Skule answered without looking at her, for he thought that if he did not meet her glance she would have no power over him.

"Are you afraid that someone is going to take that old hut? Why, the whole of Greenland is filled with Norsemen's huts that nobody wants! Come, tell me whom you are guarding it against?" Bera asked.

"Egil has said that no one may enter here except Ingeborg, and she is already inside," Kolben said and shook his spear to frighten the girl.

"You are a fool, Kolben Gode," Bera declared. "And so are you, Skule. One of these days I am going to cast a spell on you both and make your ears fall off."

As the girl walked away Kolben Gode put his hands up to his ears and Skule, whose ears could have been diminished without harming his looks, spat after her.

Bera heard her brother before she saw him. She was coming along the side of the church, and by the corner she waited and listened.

"I want you to know, Leif Magnusson, that it is I who rule at Brattahlid." Egil was about to say more but Leif interrupted him.

"I thought it was my mother's cousin Gunner Ulfson who owned Brattahlid," he said.

"Aye, so it is." Egil smiled. "But Gunner Ulfson has made me leader of his hird, I am his favorite." The last words were said mockingly.

"We have no need of hirds here in Greenland. Hirds are for earls and kings who need armies and guards." Leif paused, but as Egil said nothing he went on. "We Norsemen have only one enemy here, but he is greater than the giants of old. Winter is our enemy — the cold, the ice, the snow, are the foes we have to fight. If you will do battle against them together with us from Isa-fjord, then we offer you our friendship."

"We have other enemies as well, we have those who set themselves up against us, those who will not acknowledge our rights. Those who will not give offerings to the gods."

At this point Bera stepped out from her hiding place. Her brother saw her and, still speaking to Leif, said, "One man rules here at Brattahlid, and no one shall set himself up against him unpunished."

Those last words were meant for me, Bera thought and laughed, but this time her laughter sounded different from when the little sparrow had been its cause.

"I shall let you know" — Leif glanced at Teit and Asgrim — "what we at Isafjord think of the changes at Brattahlid." Leif turned to go, but bowed first to Bera. As he walked away he half expected to receive one of the spears between his shoulder blades, but nothing worse than a gibe from Egil was cast after him: "Be careful that you are not known as Leif the Unlucky!" As he headed for the path home, he heard Teit and Asgrim laughing behind him.

13

Ravn Eriksen

As soon as Leif returned to Isafjord he searched for Odd to discuss what had happened at Brattahlid. But Odd had not returned. Finally he asked Bjarne, Flose, and Ulv to meet him at their "hall," where he explained carefully everything that had taken place and what he thought would be the likely result for all who lived at Isafjord. As he had expected, they had very little helpful advice, except for Ulv, who suggested that someone visit one of the most distant farms, where three boys lived, two of whom were of an age to be of help.

"They live here on Isafjord," Ulv said. "I know them, for they are my cousins on my father's side. Their farm is on the second bay toward the sea."

"They have been here twice that I can remember," Leif said and laughed. "I spoke to one of them, a boy of my own age, and asked him how many sheep they had. He did not answer, but the next morning as they were leaving he came up to me and told me the exact number of their beasts. By that time I had forgotten that I had ever asked him!"

"Aye, he had to think before he answered." Ulv grinned. "It was a good thing that he managed to speak, or he would still be wondering what he should say. They chew each word five times before they spit it out."

"And because of that they never have to swallow them," Flose remarked, giving his brother a none too friendly glance.

Ulv volunteered to pay his cousins a visit to find out if they would support Leif, should it come to a battle between Isafjord and Brattahlid. But even if they should come to his aid, Leif felt far from confident. There were more people living on Eriksfjord; besides, Egil had the boat and could sail to Gardar, possibly picking up some youngsters there to join him. In spite of the loyalty of his little hird, Leif grew disheartened.

"I would give in to him," Leif later explained to his uncle Ravn, "if that served any purpose. But I could not bow low enough to suit Egil, unless I bowed myself into the grave."

"You will need the sword." Ravn Eriksen sighed. "I never learned to use it." He looked toward the corner of the hall where he kept the weapon. "I liked the old tales and they were bloody enough. My father's uncle — he had a limp — used to tell them to us in the long winter nights."

"About Erik the Red and Leif?" the boy asked.

"Oh, about them too, but I liked the tales from Iceland best, Njal's Saga and the story of Egil the Bald. The old man told them in such a manner that I thought it had all happened to him. He described the feuds, fights, and battles so well that I am not sure he himself was not under the illusion of having partaken in them." Ravn Eriksen smiled. "I have grown old, I start out in one direction and end up in another. You came for advice, not to listen to an old man's tales, which always travel backward."

"Oh, I like to hear about the old times for, surely, they were better than ours." Leif looked fondly at his uncle, then shook his head as he recalled his own troubles. "Egil will not be satisfied until he rules us all and he will be a hard master. He has taken the church away from Olaf, and he is sacrificing beasts to Odin and Thor."

"I thought of doing that once." Ravn Eriksen snorted with disgust. "It was when I was still young enough to dream. I said to myself, we have made a mistake in worshipping the White Christ. Odin and Thor are our gods and if we sacrifice to them everything will be as it was in the old times in Greenland."

"And did you?" Leif asked.

Ravn Eriksen laughed. "I did, I found a stone big enough for an altar and killed a poor lamb. But then I felt terribly ashamed."

"Why?" Leif looked attentively at his uncle.

"Because" — Ravn Eriksen paused and smiled — "because it was foolish. Those gods fitted our ancestors, who were always running off in all directions to fight and kill. But a poor farmer at the end of the world with only a few goats he can call his own, and no ability to swing a sword, is better off with Christ. What do you think Odin and Thor would think of me if they found out that I cannot even kill a snow hare?"

"Do you think Egil would leave us alone here at Isafjord if I went away?" Leif asked.

"I doubt it from what you have told me. And where would you go?"

"Nowhere." But then Leif thought of Odd, and almost said he could go and live with the little people.

"Learn to use the sword, and if Egil is so fond of Thor and Odin and the old times, dare him to single combat as they did then. We have a little island here at Isafjord that would do." Ravn Eriksen slapped the table with the flat of his hand. "I doubt if you will find him willing to come."

"Why would we need an island?" Leif asked.

"Don't you know?" His uncle sounded surprised. "In those old tales when two men disagreed about something — a woman, the border of their land, or the ownership of some beast — they would dare each other to meet on some tiny islet to fight in single combat. The reason for fighting on an island was that neither could flee. Two men walked on but only one came back." Ravn Eriksen rose, fetched the sword, and placed it on the table in front of the boy.

Leif looked at it but did not take it up, though his hand was drawn to its hilt. When he finally touched the sword he merely put it beside him on the bench, as if it were not of any great importance.

"Have you talked to your father," Ravn asked, "and told him what happened at Brattahlid?"

Leif nodded. He had, but he was not sure that his father had understood him. His mother had certainly not, for she acted merely as if Egil were some kind of bad child who deserved a beating. He tried to explain this to his uncle, but faltered several times as he realized how little help Magnus or his mother could be to him in his troubles. "They do not understand," he kept repeating.

"How could they understand?" Ravn Eriksen replied. "I am not sure that I can understand it myself. He was robbed of his hay by children, yet when he was a youngster he hardly dared open his mouth to breathe while his father was in the hall. You have always been a good son." Ravn held up his hand as Leif protested. "You have at least always pretended to do what your father asked, and Magnus has never expected more or cared. All he wants is to be allowed to dream of the royal ship from Norway that will come and carry him back to that country in glory." Ravn Eriksen smiled bitterly. "My brother is already dead, and so am I, all we want is not to be disturbed in our graves."

"I understand." Leif rose and picked up the sword. "But by right it should be he, not I, who carries this."

"And by right it should be Gunner Ulfson who came to steal our hay, not a boy unable to grow a beard." Ravn Eriksen stood up. "What help I can I shall try to give," he said and held out his hand.

Leif grasped his uncle's hand and held it in his for a moment, then walked from the hall carrying the sword under his arm like a stick.

When he went home to his father's hall he found Magnus Eriksen digging a hole in the stamped earthen floor with the only iron axe they had. Beside him stood the little wooden box where Magnus kept his silver coins.

"That is more worth stealing than any hay!" he said, his eyes shining and a cunning smile on his face.

Leif watched his father's wild chopping without saying a word, hoping that there would be no stones in the ground to damage the axe. At last the hole was deep enough. Magnus Eriksen placed the little chest in it and swept the earth back to cover it.

14

The Little People

LEIF DECIDED that a guard should be posted in the mountain pass until winter to keep a watch on what was happening at Brattahlid and to give warning should Egil decide to send out another raiding party.

But time passed and nothing happened. Odd still did not return and Bjarne said that he would not be surprised if his brother never came back, for he had often declared that one day he would live with the little people and become one of them. This made Leif eager to seek him out, for he feared that when the little people decided to move camp Odd might go with them. He waited for the return of Ulv, who had gone to visit his cousins, for he felt that of all the boys at Isafjord only Odd and Ulv could be trusted with responsibility.

Ulv was in high humor when he returned and the news he brought was good. He had explained to his cousins what had taken place at Brattahlid, and what the consequences could be for the people at Isafjord. They had listened to him but at first had said nothing. He had been well fed and given a place to sleep in their hall — and a chance, as he said, to listen in silence to the noises they made while they ate. An evening would pass without more than ten words being exchanged among them, and those were only of the most necessary kind.

"Their tongues are as unused as a newborn child's," Ulv declared. On his third day there the oldest of the brothers had taken him aside and said, "Tell Leif that if he needs us we will come." That was such an enormous effort of speechmaking that Ulv doubted if his cousin would utter another word before spring. Leif could not help laughing at the thought of Ulv, whose tongue was never still, in the same house with his dour and silent kinsmen. Ulv also brought the news that he had seen Odd but had not spoken to him, since he was in the company of two little people. He could tell Leif where to find their camp, it was not far from his cousins' farm, at the outmost point of a small peninsula.

"Do your cousins know them?" Leif asked. "Are they friendly?"

"My youngest cousin, who talks a bit more than the other two, said, 'We nod to each other.' I didn't ask him if they were friendly nods." Ulv grinned. "I will come with you if you want to visit them," he suggested.

"No, I want you here," Leif said and explained about

the posting of a guard in the pass. He flattered Ulv by putting him in charge of the others, though in truth he was glad to have an excuse for going alone. Ulv's constant chatter was like the sound of a mountain stream — lovely to listen to for a while, but soon tiresome and monotonous.

Leif set out early in the morning, carrying only a woolen blanket, his spear, and a small pouch containing some smoked mutton and goat's cheese. He took along the spear more to impress Ulv's cousins, or any of the little people he might meet, than for any other purpose. It was too heavy for throwing and would be useless in hunting hares or birds.

He rested and ate by a small lake whose water was deep and clear. One of those tiny birds called Odin's hens was swimming not far from the shore, uttering a strange, short cry. It came closer and closer, inspecting the boy. Leif made a noise and the bird flew away, only to circle the lake and come right back to land in the same spot. Even the animals in Greenland are so few, Leif thought, that they hardly know fear of each other. A fury at Egil came over him. It all seemed so unnecessary. There was nothing to fight over, there was too much land as it was. Leif had tried training with the sword, but felt silly swinging the weapon and soon gave up practicing. The idea of challenging Egil to single combat had pleased him at first, for there seemed something noble about it. But then the thought that Egil would refuse, or merely laugh at him, made him abandon the plan.

It was past noon when he arrived at the farm, which was merely a collection of huts. Ulv's cousins greeted him and bid him step inside their hall. There he met their mother, who had been a widow for nearly five years. Roald, the oldest of the boys, was nineteen and had been master of the farm since his father's death. The old woman brought a bowl of sheep's milk, which Leif drank while he explained his errand.

He was careful not to voice his fear that Odd might desert the Norse colony to share the life of the little people, as he thought that might earn the boy their contempt. Once, far to the north of Eriksfjord, he had been told, another Norse colony had been destroyed by the little people. It was so long ago that few could remember the right or the wrong of it, but some said that the Norsemen had raided the little people's camp and had taken their women as slaves. Whether the little people's revenge was justified or not, the result was that few Norsemen had come nearer to them than the distance you can cast a spear. "The eagle and falcon fly in the same sky," Leif's father had said, "but they build their nests apart."

"You will find him out by the bay near the two islets. Follow the shore and you can't miss him," Roald grunted and then added, "He is a friend of the little people. Once we traded a sheep with them for some seal meat and blubber for our lamps, but we seldom see them." This was said, Leif thought, to let him know how they felt.

The youngest brother, who had been silent, added so that it could not be misunderstood, "We do not go to their camp nor do they come here, but we meet halfway where we have built a cairn. They let us alone and we let them be."

"We are so few now," Leif said, "that it would be foolish to make them our enemies."

"Underneath a stone on top of the cairn, they put a piece of skin and we a rag if we wish to speak with each other. It is the best way," Roald grunted again. "A raven and a gull do not mate."

Leif could not help smiling on hearing his father's re-mark repeated. He left his blanket in their hall and took only his spear, saying he would return before sunset to spend the night with them if there was room.

Roald walked outside with him to point the way. Leif thought the young man had something to say to him, for his forehead was furrowed. Finally he blurted out, "Our hall is small, but large enough to house a friend." Then he turned on his heel and was gone before Leif could make a suitable reply.

As Leif made his way along the shore he followed a path made by sheep, and when that no longer went in the direction he wanted to go he struck out for a little hillock from which he would have a view of the bay. Here he discovered the cairn, but there were neither woolen rags nor skin underneath the stone. He smiled at the idea and wondered who — the Norsemen or the little people — went most often to look for a message.

Out on the fjord he saw two of the little people's boats. They were strange craft, from where he stood they looked like chips of wood floating on the sea. He had never seen one up close, but he knew they were covered by sealskins, rowed with a double oar, and terribly fragile, yet the little people hunted both whales and walruses in them. Leif was so eager to examine one that he started to run, though soon the ground became too rough. A small ridge cut across the land so he lost sight of the two kayaks.

When he saw them again, standing on a little bluff overlooking the water, they were close to the shore and to his surprise he realized that one was manned by Odd. He waved his arms and shouted his friend's name. When Odd saw him he pointed with his oar to a little pebble beach. By the time Leif made his way there the kayaks were drawn up on land and Odd and his companion were waiting.

The three boys stood for a moment looking at each other, then Odd made some strange sounds, pointing at the same time at Leif. The boy who had been in the other kayak, Leif guessed, was the same age as Odd and himself. He was not small, a tiny bit taller than Odd and very squarely built, but still he looked strange, especially his eyes, which were narrower and farther apart — a little like Bera's, Leif thought.

When Odd had finished speaking the boy grinned. When Leif asked Odd what he had said, his friend laughed and said that he had called him chief of all Norsemen and the greatest hunter among them. The boy from the little people had been staring at Leif's spear, and Leif held it out. The boy took the spear in his hand and balanced it as if he were going to cast it, then returned it, saying something in his language. "He says it is too heavy for him, and that you must be very strong," Odd explained. "He thinks you hunt the white bear with it."

"Are they difficult to row?" Leif pointed to the kayaks.

"Not once you learn how." Odd looked affectionately at the craft he had been in. "You must let it become part of you, as if you and the kayak are one, then you cannot do wrong. It is not like rowing in the boat at Brattahlid, it's more as if you yourself have become a boat."

Leif would dearly have liked to have tried one of the kayaks, but no one suggested it and he was too proud to ask. Instead he turned to Odd and said that he had something of importance to discuss. Though the boy of the little people would not have understood one word of what they said, the two boys moved a little up the beach. Leif told Odd what had happened at Brattahlid, how Egil had taken command, and that Odin and Thor were worshipped there once more.

"He knows but the names," Odd said. "Though I

think Christ, too, is dead in Greenland. There is no man alive today who has been baptized by a priest."

"And what do they believe in, what strange god have they?" Leif asked, nodding in the direction of the boy.

"I am not sure they have any god like Christ or Odin and Thor. But they believe in spirits, of animals as well as of men. I do not understand all they say."

"Will you go away with them?" Leif's voice shook with tension and he almost whispered, "I will need you."

"What you have told me should make me leave Isafjord forever, for when fools fight even a wise man can get a bloody nose." Odd glanced back to the kayak and his friend. "The sun has been a long time setting for the Norsemen and there is no reason to think it will ever rise again."

"Still, your brother and your parents are at Isafjord."

"Did he tell you that my friends here smell of whale oil?" Odd grinned. "We may both have been born from the same mother, but I do not love Bjarne, and for his sake I would not walk as far as my shadow is cast at noon on a summer day."

"So you will not come?" Leif picked up a pebble from the beach, scrutinized it, then threw it away.

"Do not make up my mind for me, I said I do not know. Maybe I will spend one more winter at Isafjord." Odd rose and walked back toward the kayaks. "If I have not come by nightfall of the day after tomorrow I shall not return."

"Please!" Leif grabbed his hand. "We are in need of you. Sometimes a wise man has to stick his nose in where fools may bloody it."

Odd laughed. "If I come it will not be because of wisdom, but because if I don't I will be wondering forever what happened."

"Whatever reason you come, you shall be welcome," Leif called as he watched the two boys launch their kayaks. As he was about to set out for the homeward trek he glanced toward the camp of the little people. At the end of the beach a lone figure stood watching him — a girl. Leif raised his hand and waved, but the girl did not wave back. She shifted her glance to the two boys in the kayaks, who by now were well out on the blue waters of the fjord. For some reason he could not explain, Leif felt certain that the one she was watching was Odd.

15

Ingeborg

NEAR THE southwest corner of the churchyard at Brattahlid was a little grass-covered mound with a wooden cross on top. Here lay Gudrin Sigridsdaughter, Ingeborg's mother. There was no name carved on the cross, it was just two pieces of wood roughly fastened together. In the summer when the weather was warm, Ingeborg would visit the grave, bringing little gifts of flowers plucked in the fields. She had no memory of Gudrin Sigridsdaughter, only a burning longing and desire to have a mother, like everyone else she knew. She was doubly aware of her loss because her father could not provide that warmth and protection which a mother gives a small child. In his way Gunner Ulfson loved his daughter, and had never raised his hand to her, even when some might have thought he had reason to do so. But he was a weak man, a failure at all he had attempted, and like many such men he was concerned not to appear unmanly. Unfortunately for Ingeborg, he thought that showing any kind of affection, even for his motherless child, was the mark of a weakling. Her father's servant, Astrid, was all the mother Ingeborg had ever known, and she was too submissive to do much more than spoil her, agreeing with her every wish, making them into commands if she could fulfill them.

On that very day when Leif set out after Odd, Ingeborg decorated her mother's grave with the last of the fall flowers. She braided a garland of buttercups and hung them around the cross. Sitting on the mound she wondered, as she had so many times before, what her mother had looked like. Astrid had said she was beautiful, but Ingeborg was clever enough to know that Astrid always said what she thought would please her. As a tiny child Ingeborg used to talk to her mother, telling that wooden cross all her sorrows and sometimes, though much more rarely, her joys as well. Now, almost a young woman, she spoke again, asking questions as she had done as a child.

"Oh, Mother, why does Father let Egil rule? That boy makes fun even of Father and shows his contempt for him. Why, anyone would think that Egil was chieftain of Brattahlid. No one shows any respect for Father anymore, except Thorkil, and he doesn't matter." The girl plucked a few blades of grass that grew on the grave and tore them to pieces. "If I were Father," she whispered, "I would take my big sword and kill Egil." She paused for a moment, then nodding furiously she said, "I would!"

"Ingeborg!" A voice called and the girl looked up. Atle was standing near her. Of all Astrid's children Atle was dearest to her. Ingeborg and Atle had been together often when young and his mother had spoiled them both.

"What do you want?" Ingeborg's voice was not friendly.

"Your uncle Olaf is not well." Atle took one step nearer.

"That is no news. How could he be? Your master, Egil, has taken his church away from him." The girl frowned.

"He is not my master," Atle said sourly.

"He is not mine either and he never will be," Ingeborg snorted. "I spit on him!" she exclaimed and spat. Some of the spittle ran down her chin and made it necessary for her to wipe it, which subtracted from the impressiveness of the act.

Atle sat down on a grave mound nearby. "He is going to sacrifice another sheep in a day or two. We are all going to dip our weapons in the blood on the altar."

"Why does my father let him?" Ingeborg looked at the comrade of her childhood. "Tell me, Atle!"

The appeal in her voice made the boy uncomfortable. Instead of answering, he repeated the message he had come with. "Your uncle is not well."

"We have always been friends." The girl's voice shook.

"Has Ingeborg Gudrinsdaughter not a friend left at Brattahlid?" she asked.

"I am your friend and your uncle's too." Atle looked down at his hands, which lay folded in his lap. "Egil has promised your father all of Magnus Eriksen's silver." The boy looked up. "You know your father will do anything for that."

"And how will he get Magnus Eriksen's silver?" Ingeborg asked.

Atle shrugged his shoulders. "The same way that he got his hay," he finally replied.

"He got that when there were only a few old men at Isafjord. Leif was away, or he might have found that it was not so easy for a thief to steal."

"We shall have twice as many men as Leif has." Atle sounded belligerent again.

"You have never liked him," Ingeborg said softly. "When we were children and Leif came, you refused to play and would go somewhere to sulk."

"Does that matter?" Atle looked at Ingeborg. "But you may be right, whenever he came I felt like the servants' child."

"That wasn't his fault," Ingeborg pleaded. "He never meant you to feel that way."

"No." Atle smiled. "That is true, it was his appearance, his way of acting as if he were chieftain by God's will."

"That was not Leif's doing." Ingeborg turned her back on Atle for a moment to look out over the fjord. "It was yours. It was envy in your eyes that made you see crooked. Whatever he did you thought it wrong."

"Have you ever considered, Inge " — Atle called her by the name she had given herself when she first learned to talk — "what it feels like to know that your own mother, and father as well, think more of someone else's children than of their own? Once when I was young I threw a stone at Leif. I did not even hit him, but my mother saw it and beat me."

"And so she should have." Ingeborg turned back to look at him. "You deserved it."

"Ah, but you see I knew that I was not being beaten for having thrown the stone." Atle lifted his hand and pointed a finger at the girl. "I was being beaten for having thrown it at Leif, the son of the master at Isafjord, and that hurt far more than the blows."

"And you remember that now, so many years after." Ingeborg spoke contemptuously. "You have a slave's soul."

An expression went across Atle's face as if he had been struck. He clenched his fist so hard that the knuckles went white, then slowly his hands and the muscles in his face relaxed. "Your uncle needs you, he is sick, go to him," he said and rose.

When Ingeborg entered the little hut where her uncle Olaf had made his home she stood by the open door and spoke his name. She could see a tuft of black hair sticking out from underneath the skins and woolen blanket that covered him. When he did not answer she closed the door behind her and walked over to his couch on tiptoe.

"Uncle Olaf," she whispered, "Uncle Olaf." She touched his hair and stroked it gently. "It is I, Ingeborg, little Inge," she said, speaking as one would to a frightened child.

With difficulty Olaf Ulfson turned to look at his niece. "Ingeborg," he sighed and smiled, drawing his hand out from under the covers to catch hold of hers.

Olaf Ulfson's hand was cold as if it belonged more to the grave than to life. Gently Ingeborg rubbed it between her warm young hands.

"I have had a terrible dream of ill omens," Olaf said, looking at the girl sitting at his bedside. "I dreamt that I was living in those dark times before Christ came to earth, and I was to be offered to those terrible gods like —" Olaf sighed — "like a sheep."

"No one will do that to you." Ingeborg smiled at her uncle. "You shouldn't have dreams like that," she said, as if we are rulers of that world which opens up to us when we close our eyes.

"It wasn't death that was so terrible, I have long yearned for that. No, it was the shame I felt when I knew . . ."

"When you knew what?" the girl asked.

"That I was afraid of the pain." Her uncle closed his eyes but kept on talking. "You see, it was because of Him, because I was a Christian, that I was to be offered." With a childish candor, Olaf Ulfson opened his eyes. "That happened often in the old times, I have been told of that." Her uncle closed his eyes again and repeated, "But I was afraid of the pain." Then as if he were confessing he said, "And that is a sin, for if you are dying for Him then you should not fear the pain but long for it, and I didn't!"

On the last word Olaf's voice broke and the girl thought that her uncle would cry. She quickly said, "But Uncle, it was only a dream, and dreams don't matter. I have dreams, some of them strange. In one I was chased by a white bear, and don't think I wasn't frightened then." Olaf Ulfson smiled and Ingeborg hurried on. "I told it to Astrid and she thinks she knows what dreams mean. But what she said was all nonsense, about a man I was to marry, and everyone knows I am going to marry Leif."

When Olaf heard Leif's name mentioned he asked if he had been to Brattahlid lately and why he had not come to see him.

"He is very busy, his father is no help to him," Ingeborg lied. "I am sure he will come as soon as the first snow falls."

"You know what I dreamt too?" Olaf Ulfson smiled bashfully, as if he were about to part with a secret dear to him.

"No!" The girl smiled too and looked like a young mother sitting at the bedside of her child. "But I would like to know," she said encouragingly.

"I dreamt that the bishop came!" Her uncle wrinkled his brow. "It must be next year he is coming, for it was summer." Olaf hesitated and then smiled again. "The sail had a golden cross and the bishop himself stood on the starboard side holding the big oar in his hand. His cape was red like the setting sun in winter and in his hand he had a golden staff. The ship landed right here at Brattahlid and, you know, when my grandfather was a child the bell from the church was melted down, but in my dream I heard it ring." Olaf Ulfson shook his head slightly, in wonder at his own tale.

"What happened then, Uncle?" Ingeborg asked.

"Then he came right up here and he asked for me. I kneeled in front of him, and he touched me with his golden staff and said I was a priest. The weather was so warm, like the summers when I was a child. Gudrin was there too and she clapped her hands when the bishop made me a priest."

Ingeborg stroked her uncle's hand gently; while she watched his worn face, a tear ran down his cheek. He has not been washed for weeks, she thought, but it does not matter, for there are no summers left for him. She sat at the bedside a long, long time, until her uncle fell asleep.

16

A Visit to Brattahlid

I F I AM not there by nightfall on the day after tomorrow then I shan't ever come back to Isafjord." Leif recalled Odd's words as he sat watching for the boy. He glanced at the sun, it would soon be setting. They have given him the kayak, and he won't come, he thought.

When he finally saw Odd silhouetted against the sky as he emerged on the summit of a small hill he could hardly believe his eyes.

"I didn't think you would come!" he shouted as he ran to meet him.

"Yesterday I did not either, but then I had a dream that commanded me to go." Odd laughed good-naturedly.

"A lucky dream!" Leif held out his hand.

"For whom?" Odd took Leif's hand. "For you or for me?"

"For both of us, I hope." From where the two boys stood they could see the houses at Isafjord. From Magnus Eriksen's hall a thin stream of smoke was rising. "Tomorrow I want to go to Brattahlid. Will you come with me?" Leif asked.

"I will." Odd nodded in the direction he had come from. "I have found some driftwood," he said.

"We will fetch that later. Unless you think we should get it first?"

"The wood will keep, it is not far away," Odd said. "I and a . . . a friend collected it and made a float that we towed with our kayaks. Where do you think that timber comes from?"

"I don't know, some say it comes from the country of the setting sun, the one that Leif, son of Erik, visited." The boy suddenly remembered that Egil had called him Leif the Unlucky. I must dub him something that will bring him shame, he thought.

"How many of us shall go to Brattahlid?" Odd glanced at his friend, they were near the house now.

"Just you and me, I think. We shall go on a peaceful errand." Leif looked out over the fjord. The sun was just setting, painting the tips of the icebergs red like blood. "I think we shall go unarmed," he added.

The days were no longer as warm as they had been in the summer, and from sunset to sunrise a man could get a good sleep. It was not winter yet and the grass was still summer green. The two boys had set out just before sunrise, the snow-covered mountains in the east were already pink. As they reached the pass to Brattahlid the sun rose and the pale sky turned blue. Few places in the world are more beautiful than Greenland and, even though Leif and Odd had never seen any other parts of the world, for a moment they stood in awe looking down over Eriksfjord and the mountains to the south toward Gardar.

"When there was a bishop in Gardar they say that a watch was kept on one of the mountains during the summer, to tell if any ship were in the offing. They say there is a small hut up there," Leif said, shielding his eyes with his hand as he tried to make out on which peak the watchtower had been.

"I wonder if Egil has set a watch to see if we are in the offing." Odd carried no weapon, but both boys had stout sticks in their hands that might do very well if it came to a fight.

"I think he has, so it is just as well we do not try to hide, but walk straight down the usual path." Leif smiled. "We shall act once more as if we were friends, even though it is of little use."

"Look!" Odd pointed up into the sky. Two eagles were circling above Brattahlid. "The other day I saw a falcon. I would like to find its nest and steal one of its young to train for hunting."

"The Greenland falcon was thought a royal gift in Norway, worth its weight in silver." Leif laughed. "Maybe someday a ship will come to fetch some falcons, or maybe they no longer hunt with them and that is why no ship comes."

"Or maybe there are no longer any kings, and there is no need for falcons, no need for royal gifts," Odd suggested.

"There will always be kings, and if there aren't, then they will just call themselves something else, but it will always be the same." Leif's tone of voice was bitter. "There will always be an Egil."

"And will he always win?" Odd asked. The two boys were now near the buildings of Brattahlid.

"No." Leif stood still. "He won't always win, but he will cause trouble and pain enough." Leif lowered his voice. "Another winter like the one we had four years ago when half the sheep of Isafjord and Brattahlid died, and we will die with the beasts. There are so many things we should do, but Egil keeps us from doing them." The boy sighed like an old man. "I would let him rule if there were any sense to what he wants to do." Leif looked at his friend. "I don't care, Odd, *who* calls himself chieftain."

"Is that what you have come to offer him?" Odd asked. "If it is, I think he will tell you that it is not for you to give. He is the kind of person who only feels that something is his if he has taken it. If you offer him the chieftainship of Brattahlid he will think himself insulted."

Leif bit his lip gently. "I know he hates me and we shall never be friends, but I shall keep out of his way if only he will do some of those things that must be done."

Odd laughed. "If only he will do what you tell him, then he can be chieftain? I think it will be wise of you not to tell him that."

Leif shook his head. "I shan't put it like that. We have come to see my mother's cousin Olaf, I have heard he is not well. Look!" A boy and a girl had come from the hall and were walking toward them. "It is Skule and Gunhild and I don't think either of them is my friend."

"What brings you to Brattahlid?" Skule had the disturbing habit of not looking at the person he was speaking to but at some point slightly to the right, as if a ghost, invisible to all but himself, were standing there.

"I have heard that my cousin Olaf is sick and I have come to see him."

"He is dying," Gunhild said.

"Where is he?" Leif asked abruptly. "In the hall?"

"Over there." Skule nodded in the general direction. "But Egil has said that no one is to visit him."

"And where is Egil?" It was with difficulty that Leif kept calm.

"He has gone somewhere with Kolben and my brother, Atle, I don't know where." In his confusion Skule glanced even farther askew, as if the invisible ghost had moved.

"I am sure that Olaf Ulfson would like to see me," Odd said, his voice calm but a little threatening. "Get out of my way, Skule, and take your sister with you."

For a moment it looked as though it might come to a fight, but then Skule realized that if it did he would be the one to receive the beating. "I have only repeated Egil's orders," he mumbled as he walked away.

Ingeborg, sitting at her uncle's bedside, turned as the door to the hut was thrown open. Seeing Leif and Odd, she smiled and beckoned them to come in. "He is asleep," she whispered, standing up so that Leif could see his mother's cousin.

So clearly had death marked Olaf Ulfson's face that Leif knew immediately he would never be well again. The dying man drew his breath with such difficulty that the boy felt that it could stop at any moment. He wanted to kneel and pray, but he didn't know any prayers. The crude cross that had been hanging in the church now decorated the wall of the hut. Leif looked at it and made the sign of the cross over the sleeping man. Not until then did he notice that there was someone else in the room. Bera was crouching in a corner staring at him intently.

"Come outside where we can talk," Ingeborg whispered and made a sign to Bera that she should take over her post at the bedside.

"He will not live much longer." As Ingeborg said the

words she felt ashamed, for the thought of her uncle's death was a relief. She had sat by his deathbed for the last three days, only allowing herself a few hours of sleep when her eyes refused to stay open.

"When did it happen?" Leif asked foolishly, as if sickness were like an accident that has both time and place.

"He has been coughing all summer, and grown thin." Ingeborg looked down toward the fjord as if she was searching for someone. "But it was after Egil took his church that he went to bed and would not get up."

"What right had Egil to take his church?" Leif shouted. Ingeborg put a finger in front of her mouth and begged him to be quiet.

"Whatever right the strong have over the weak," she said. "He was the last Christian in Greenland, even my father did not go to the church anymore."

"Does your father bow to Egil's gods now?" Leif kept his voice low, but it was no less angry.

"He does." Ingeborg nodded. "You did not come to the church either, Leif."

"I know." Leif touched Ingeborg's shoulder. "But I loved my cousin Olaf."

"So did I," the girl whispered. "He was more my father than Gunner ever was."

Suddenly Leif remembered his mother's words and wished passionately that the dying man might have heard what his niece had said. "Did you ever tell him that?" he asked.

"I did not have to, he knew." Ingeborg smiled, but her smile vanished suddenly and she pointed down the fjord to where Gunner Ulfson's boat could be seen coming toward Brattahlid. "You must not be here when he comes back."

"And who is *he?*" Leif looked toward the boat.

"Egil," Ingeborg answered. "He has sworn that he will kill you if you come to Brattahlid."

"I thought your father was chieftain here, not the son of a man who hardly knows who his grandfather was," Leif snarled, not noticing the frown on Odd's face.

"Egil is stronger than my father and he plays up to him, letting him think that it is he who gives the orders." Ingeborg was still following the boat with her eyes. "You must go before they land, you are only two and they are many."

"And what about you? Come to Isafjord with me. Now!"

"I cannot leave my uncle." Ingeborg turned to go back into the hut. "But I will not be Egil's wife."

"His wife!" Leif screamed, and again the girl put her finger to her mouth to quiet him.

"He wants to marry me and my father has given his word, but that will not happen." Ingeborg smiled like someone who has a secret that no one else knows.

"But he cannot, you have been promised to me!" Leif said. Such was his contempt for Egil that it had never entered his mind that Egil could desire Ingeborg.

"*Cannot* is a word that Egil does not know." Ingeborg shook her head. "But he shall be taught it," she said, as her hand grasped the latch of the door. "But now you must go back to Isafjord. I shall send a messenger, if you keep a watch in the pass."

"Can you trust her?" Leif nodded toward the hut and Bera who was inside. "After all, she is his sister."

"I can trust her." Ingeborg smiled. "And so can you, I think." With those words she opened the door and slid inside.

"Shall we wait for him?" Leif nodded toward the boat, which was now near the shore. "He will not think us cowards if we don't?"

"He might," Odd said. "But better to be live cowards than dead heroes."

"I wish him dead." Leif turned and walked toward the path that led to Isafjord.

Odd, who was still watching the boat, whispered to himself, "And so does he, and so does he."

17

The Rescue of Ulv

FATHER!"

Magnus Eriksen looked at his son, who had just entered the hall and was calling him. Leif will soon be a man, he thought to himself. The thought gave him little pleasure.

"And what do you want?" he asked, recalling that when he was Leif's age he had wanted so much.

"Somebody must go and talk to Gunner Ulfson. I have tried." Leif sat down at the table, his hands gently touching its veined surface black with age. More than three hundred years ago its planks had been brought from Norway. "You must tell him that there must be peace between us at Isafjord and the people of Brattahlid."

"Why do you think he will listen to me?" Magnus smiled. "Or, for that matter, to your mother?"

"I don't know if he would listen to you and if he did

whether he would have the power to do much, but I want no stone unturned beneath which hope might have hidden." Leif looked at his father and thought, He is an old man.

"Leif, I think the boats from Norway are coming soon, only one more winter will we have to wait and then . . ." Magnus Eriksen made a motion with his hands to signify the glory that would then be theirs.

Leif glanced with disgust at his father. "You are afraid to go."

"I have hidden my silver, they shan't find it." Magnus winked. "It is yours too."

"I wonder if Mother would go. After all, Gunner is her kin." Leif mumbled so low that he was surprised when his father answered.

"They hated each other as children and always fought. Sometimes your mother gave him a beating," he added with glee.

"If we gave him your silver he might leave us alone," Leif suggested, knowing full well what his father's reaction would be.

"No!" Magnus Eriksen could not help but look toward that point on the floor beneath which his treasure rested. "Some of that silver was struck by King Olaf the Great and bears his sign. It has been in our family as long as man can remember. Before I give it up to anyone born of woman, I would give up my life."

"It probably does not matter, even if one made a chain of silver I doubt if it would bind Egil." Leif shook his head as he rose and then, feeling sorry for his father, he said, "Don't worry, we will protect your silver."

He was about to go and talk to his mother when someone called him. It was Odd.

"What troubles you?" he asked, walking outside.

"Little troubles me." Odd looked up toward the pass. "But a lot troubles Ulv, he was captured and taken to Brattahlid."

"Captured?" Leif looked at Odd in amazement.

"His brother had come up to relieve him and he saw them — the three Gode brothers. They had Ulv between them and were halfway down the mountain, but not so far away that Flose could not recognize them."

"They must have surprised him, for Ulv is a fast runner and would have escaped them had he had warning." Leif felt that Ulv's capture was his fault. He should have posted two men in the pass. "We cannot afford to lose anyone," he mumbled, more to himself than to Odd. "Let us visit Brattahlid again. Tonight there is a new moon and they won't be expecting us so soon."

"Best wait until after midnight," Odd replied. "After midnight ghosts rise from the graves, and then those who fear them like to stay in their beds and hide beneath their covers."

"Just you and me." Leif held out his hand and Odd silently shook it.

A little snow had fallen that day, but by evening the sky was clear and all the stars shone. By the time the boys set out it was past midnight and the new moon was already setting. It was freezing but not a hard frost, and the boys kept warm by walking. Leif was carrying his spear and his knife, Odd the light spear he used for fishing and the one iron axe of Isafjord.

"If they have set a guard over him it will probably be Skule or Gunhild," Leif explained. "Neither the Gode brothers nor Atle would want their sleep interrupted."

"They might have tied him up inside the hall," Odd suggested.

"I doubt that. This is Egil's work and I do not think even Gunner knows of it. I hope the dogs will not bark." Leif smiled. "Or, for that matter, wag their tails — one of them is a pup from Isafjord."

"How many dogs have they?" Odd asked and sniffed. He was catching a cold.

"I think three. When I was a small boy we had many dogs, remember? Then in the bad winter when I was five they were all killed to save feeding them. All but a couple of bitches and one male dog. I remember crying, for I had a favorite pup that was deemed not worthy of life."

"According to my father they were eaten," Odd said, adding, "but my mother claims that wasn't true, they used the dead dogs to feed the live ones."

"My pup was the runt of the litter." Leif smiled to himself. "He was such a happy little one, always up to some trick or other. Still, they were probably right, he would have been little use as a sheepdog."

"I remember being hungry that winter, for the ewes gave no milk and there was no cheese." Odd sniffed once more. "Damn my nose!" he exclaimed. "I shall probably start sneezing as soon as we get near Brattahlid."

"Don't worry," Leif said. "Just so long as Egil doesn't wipe our noses we shall be all right."

"I would not let him wipe mine." Odd laughed.

"Let us try Olaf Ulfson's hut first," Leif whispered as they came near the buildings of Brattahlid. "They might keep Ulv there to save a watch."

But there was no guard at the hut. The boys listened at the door but all was silent. Through a crack in the wood they could see that a light was burning within. Carefully Leif lifted the latch and opened the door just enough to see inside.

His kinsman Olaf Ulfson was dead. He lay stretched out upon the bed, his hands folded in prayer on his chest, near him a single little tallow lamp burned and farther over in a corner sat Astrid, Atle and Skule's mother, sound asleep. At her feet lay a dog. It raised its head when it recognized Leif and started to wag its tail. The boy made a motion with his hand, silently calling the dog, who came cringing toward him.

As soon as Leif had closed the door again he bent down to pet the dog, for he was afraid it might bark out of sheer joy. It was the dog who had come from Isafjord as a pup. Leif knew it well, by disposition it was more of a pet than a work dog. "We shall try the church, they may keep him there," Leif whispered. Odd nodded to show that he had understood. The church had a stone fence round its graveyard, and it was possible to get quite near its door without being seen.

"There seems to be no one here either," Odd whispered.

"It is too cold to post a guard outside," Leif answered as he vaulted the fence. "Look!" He pointed to the little window. The sheep's bladder that covered it shone golden in the darkness. Once that little window had been the pride of Brattahlid, for it had been glazed with colored glass.

"Egil began this fight, but I shall not be the first to spill blood." Leif's hand was on the latch. "If we can, let us overpower them but not hurt them."

"Then the first spilled blood will be either yours or mine, I am sure," Odd argued as the dog started to growl. Leif made no reply, for he feared that the dog would have warned those inside. He threw open the door and rushed in.

Skule and Atle's sister, Gunhild, was sitting near the altar, cold to the bone. As the boys entered she jumped up, but one of her legs had been asleep and she had to sit down again.

"Close the door," Leif shouted to Odd and then, pointing his spear at the girl, he asked, "Where is Ulv?"

The girl stared at the point of the spear as if she expected it to pierce her at any moment. Finally, as if in a trance, she pointed toward a dark corner of the room.

Leif grabbed the little stone lamp that stood on the altar and lifted it carefully, for such tallow lamps are easily extinguished. Ulv lay on the ground, tied like a beast ready for slaughter, bound hand and foot and gagged as well. The ropes were of woven sealskin and very strong, so it took Leif a while to cut them. When the gag was removed Ulv whispered, "It was good you came, I fear tomorrow would have been too late."

"Why?" Leif asked, also keeping his voice low.

Ulv breathed deeply and stretched his arms, but before he could answer Odd called, "Bring the light!" Gunhild had tried to escape but he had caught her. Leif put the lamp on top of the altar, now it lit the whole room darkly. Odd sat on top of the girl holding her arms but she kicked madly. They bound her securely with the ropes that had been used to tie Ulv, but she was strong and gave so much trouble that in the end they had to gag her as well, although much against their will.

The rope had been so tight around Ulv's wrists and ankles that it had cut into his flesh. When he tried to stand up, his legs would not carry him. Odd rubbed the places where the rope had cut until the blood started to circulate freely again. "Try to stand now, lean on my shoulder," Odd suggested and, groaning, Ulv stood up.

"We must be going." Leif tested the girl's bonds to

make sure that they were no tighter than necessary and loosened her gag a little. "Someone will come and free you soon," he said as they left the church, half carrying Ulv between them.

"May she choke to death!" Ulv whispered. "She was the one who tied my gag, and laughed when it cut my mouth until it bled."

"Why did they tie you like that?" Leif asked as they paused for a moment.

"They were going to offer me!" Ulv snarled.

"Offer you?" Odd asked incredulously. "To whom?"

"To Egil's gods." Ulv looked back toward the church. "To Odin and Thor."

18

The Death of Olaf Ulfson

U NCLE OLAF is dead!" Ingeborg, who had just closed the eyes of Olaf Ulfson, whispered the words almost like a sigh. Gunner Ulfson felt depressed, for he had just returned from the beach where he had watched the first thin layer of ice forming on the water near the shore. Each year the coming of winter extinguished all his hopes, and his dreams became nightmares. Not before midwinter had passed would his expectations be reborn. In reality he was not sorry to hear of his brother's death, for that was one person less to have claims on him.

"When did he die?" he asked. "Was it before or after the sun rose?"

"Just at sunrise, I think." Ingeborg tried to remember, but she was not sure.

"That is a good omen. Those who die at sunrise head straight for heaven, so I have heard." Her father smiled.

It was more a grimace, but then Gunner's face was unused to smiling.

"I wanted him to be put in the church. But not now that Egil has made a slaughterhouse of it." Ingeborg tried to catch her father's eye.

"When Christ first came to Greenland and Iceland he, Thor, and Odin lived well enough together," Gunner mumbled. He had not liked Egil's making the church into a temple for the old gods, but he had not had the courage to forbid it.

"How do you know if that is the truth? It is only an old story." For some reason, while she spoke Ingeborg could hear her uncle telling of the pictures that had once decorated the walls of the church and she said, "The church belonged to Uncle Olaf, it was his!"

"Brattahlid belongs to me and no one else. So does the church, and if I want Odin worshipped as well as Christ then it is for me to decide." Gunner Ulfson sounded angrier than he was.

"I thought you had given Brattahlid to that son of a pauper from the innermost part of the fjord." Ingeborg turned contemptuously on her father. "Methinks his great-grandfather was born a slave."

"Egil is of good family, his mother, Solveig, came from a farm almost as large as ours south of Gardar, her kin came with Erik to Greenland." Gunner Ulfson, who was so proud of his ancestry, took Ingeborg's slight of Egil seriously.

"If his great-grandfather were a king and his mother a princess, I could not care less. Though I think there is more chance that he was a troll and his mother" — angrily Ingeborg stumbled as she searched for a word — "a codfish! For the blood that runs in his veins is as cold as a fish's."

"He has asked for my permission to marry you." While Gunner Ulfson watched his daughter, he thought of her mother. Ingeborg reminded him of Gudrin Sigridsdaughter. He had loved her, even though she had not cared for him.

"If you say yes," replied Ingeborg, who had been sitting on the bench in the hall at Brattahlid, but now stood up and stamped her foot, "then you can celebrate my wedding and my funeral on the same day."

"I have not yet given my answer," Gunner Ulfson snorted. "But mind me, or it will be yes."

"I will not marry Egil!" Ingeborg's voice broke in childish anger.

"You will mind me as a child should!" Gunner Ulfson rose to mark that this was the end of the conversation as far as he was concerned.

"And will Egil mind you too?" Ingeborg snapped as she turned to leave the hall.

"Why should I not mind the chieftain of Brattahlid?" a voice said from the door. It was Egil, he had stood there listening to the last part of the quarrel between father and daughter.

"Because you don't mind anyone but yourself." Ingeborg turned like a cornered animal. "I hate you, Egil Sigurdson," she spat out as she ran from the room.

"She will do what I tell her," Gunner Ulfson said unconvincingly and added, "If she doesn't, she shall be sorry."

"I am sure she will mind you, after all you are her father." Egil managed to insert a question mark at the end of the sentence, insulting the older man, but Gunner either did not notice or chose not to do so.

"When the ship from Norway comes next year," he said falteringly, "then she will understand that everything we do is for her good."

"I have sent the three Gode boys to the pass to capture whomever Leif keeps there as guard." Egil sprawled rather than sat on the bench by the table. "They should be back soon."

"I hope they have not harmed whoever was there," Gunner Ulfson said nervously, seating himself once more in the chieftain's seat.

"I know of no one who has eaten an egg without cracking its shell first." Egil grinned.

"I don't want anyone harmed at Isafjord." Gunner Ulfson tried to make his words sound like a command.

"Oh, we wouldn't like to harm anyone." Egil's voice sounded insincere.

"We will find out from our prisoner where Magnus keeps his silver." The boy watched the expression on the older man's face, and when greed appeared he smiled.

"But that silver should have been mine." Gunner's voice shook with expectation. "Magnus holds his farm under Brattahlid."

"Aye, all of Greenland is under Brattahlid, did not Erik the Red discover and call it all his own?" Egil watched Gunner Ulfson's face with the same intensity as he would have watched embers that he was blowing on a fire. "Whoever owns Brattahlid owns Greenland."

"And Brattahlid is mine." The hall was dark, so Gunner Ulfson could not see the expression on Egil Sigurdson's face. If he had, he might have been less sure of the truth of what he had said.

Ingeborg had run from the hall to find Astrid. She wanted to tell the servant of her uncle's death, but she also wanted to be comforted. Astrid was all the mother Ingeborg had ever known, she had comforted her as a small child. But Astrid had not been able to replace Gudrin Sigridsdaughter, she was much too aware that her little charge was the daughter of her master ever to show that spontaneous warmth which is the mark of a mother. She had loved Ingeborg, she had been kind and had taken good care of her, but from the time the girl had taken her first few steps and had spoken her first few words, Astrid had been her servant.

"Astrid, Uncle Olaf is dead!" As Ingeborg spoke the words for the second time that morning she was suddenly aware of their meaning, that she would never see her uncle again. Tears formed in her eyes and ran down her cheeks. Astrid, who had been to the spring for water, put the bucket down upon the ground but she hesitated before opening her arms as if unsure that that was the right thing to do. Ingeborg embraced her and for a moment hid her face against the older woman's shoulder, but it gave her no respite from her sorrow.

"Will you help me lay him out?" Ingeborg asked and Astrid nodded, grasping the handle of the bucket again.

"I shall tell Thorkil to dig a grave — lucky it is that the earth is not frozen yet." They walked toward the hall. As they drew near, Ingeborg saw her father entering his brother's hut, and it pleased her that he had gone to pay his respects to Olaf.

When Astrid and Ingeborg came to lay out the dead man Gunner Ulfson had gone. There was little to do. Ingeborg was sorry that all the flowers were already gone, but she found a few sprigs of willow that were still green and placed them by her uncle's head.

"Uncle Olaf wore a silver cross beneath his shirt, take it out so that all can see it," Ingeborg ordered, wondering if her father would speak at the grave and if she should say a prayer. This was most worrying because she did not know any, at least not any real ones. She made up her own but they were more like private conversations with God.

"There is no cross," Astrid declared. "There is a leather string but it has been broken. Look." She handed the leather strand to Ingeborg.

"It has been cut." Ingeborg blushed. Now she knew why her father had come and she turned away to hide her shame. "I will stay with Uncle Olaf if you will go and get his grave ready," she said, her voice trembling. "Tomorrow he shall be buried."

When Astrid had left Ingeborg sank on her knees beside the bed where her uncle lay. She folded her hands, wanting to pray, but all she could say, and repeat over and over again, was "I am sorry, sorry, sorry."

19

Ulv's Story

"THEY WANTED to know where your father kept his silver." For the first time since they had returned to Isafjord Ulv grinned. "I would have told them if I had known." He laughed as he explained the reason for his merriment. "I told them anyway, I said that Magnus Eriksen had dug it down underneath the hearthstone in his hall."

"Did you tell them how large the hoard was too?" Leif did not smile. By chance Ulv had made a guess that was correct within a foot or two.

"I said he had as much as two men could carry." Ulv looked from Leif to Odd, sensing that he had done wrong but not quite sure how. "That is, if they were strong," he added happily.

"My father has but a handful of silver that he thinks of great value." Leif glanced at Odd. "Do you think Egil is foolish enough to believe such a tale?"

"No." Odd shook his head. "But Gunner Ulfson might, and Egil would be the last one to dissuade him of its truth."

"Yes," Leif agreed. "It would help him convince my mother's cousin of the need to make war on us at Isafjord. Gunner Ulfson would kill his own daughter for as much silver as two men could carry." As he spoke he grew pale, for suddenly he realized what he was saying.

"Ingeborg is betrothed to him." Ulv, who was lying on his plank bed in his parents' house, looked at Leif. "So he bragged to me, but I don't think it was the truth. I don't know why I think he was lying, but I am sure he was."

"But if he got my father's silver, then . . ." Leif smiled sourly and shook his head.

"But he hasn't got it yet," Odd said, trying to sound encouraging. "And even if he did, would not Gunner Ulfson be disappointed if he found out it amounted to no more than what a tiny child could carry with ease?"

"The reason why I smiled" — Leif, who had been sitting on Ulv's bed, stood up — "is that I am beginning to realize that I will have to fight for something on which I set no value. I would use my father's bits of silver as weights on my fishing line without giving it a second thought, or trade them all for one good iron axe and think that I had got the better of the bargain . . . And now —" Leif made a motion with his hands to show his disgust.

"If it had not been your father's silver it would have been something else," Odd said. "A man who longs for a fight will not search for an excuse but will grab the first that comes."

"True, and I don't think we shall have long to wait." Leif turned to Ulv. "Can you be at our hall tomorrow?"

Ulv drew the woolen blanket that covered him up to his nose. "I am black and blue from the blows of Egil and his friends, but I have no broken bones . . . I will be there."

Leif smiled and raised his hand in a salute as he left; Odd winked at Ulv as he followed. When the two boys were well away from the house, Leif said bitterly, "If my father had shown more imagination in finding a hiding place and Ulv a little less, all might be well."

"I would rather like to see the face of Gunner Ulfson when he is told that we have as much silver in Isafjord as two men can carry," Odd said, laughing at the thought.

"I doubt if Egil will tell him that, he is not such a fool as to believe it." Leif raised his hand and shouted "Down!" to the dog, who was jumping up at him. "He won't like that we took the dog either, not that it is of any use." At his last words the dog barked happily, wagging its tail as if it agreed. "Let's go and tell my uncle Ravn," Leif suggested. "He might give us advice on what to do."

"Oh, that he will — it is the one thing everyone will give freely, but it is seldom worth taking," Odd grumbled, following Leif to his uncle's hall all the same. The dog ran behind them, not like a dog that has reached an age of discretion, but rather like a puppy that must sniff each stone it passes.

"They threatened to offer him to Odin." Leif was explaining Ulv's adventure at Brattahlid to his uncle. "They showed him the stone altar all spattered with blood. It was sheep's blood, but they told him that he would be next."

"Do you think they would have?" Ravn Eriksen looked thoughtfully at his nephew.

"No." Leif shook his head. "Ulv didn't think so either, but Gunhild, who was guarding him, did. She took a knife and put it to his throat to show him how they were going to do it. Ulv thinks it was her idea."

"When I heard it I wished I had tightened the ropes around her a little more," Odd mumbled.

"She is only a fool enjoying her power for the moment, tomorrow she will be as docile as a sheep," Leif grunted.

"When sheep have knives I don't care to be a shepherd," Odd replied. "Leif said he wanted to ask your advice. What do you counsel us to do, Ravn Eriksen?"

Ravn Eriksen looked so long at the boys before he answered that Odd felt embarrassed and glanced down at his sheepskin boots.

"If Egil, who is your own age, is the real master of Brattahlid, then you should know better than I what to do. When I was a boy our will was not our own but our parents'. We did as they said even when we thought it foolish."

"Uncle Ravn, we will do whatever you tell us to." Leif looked at his uncle as he spoke. "My father only fears for his silver, he is no master of Isafjord anymore."

Ravn Eriksen smiled and then shook his head. His servant Kark, who seldom spoke, was standing near him. "Kark, I have been offered the chieftainship of Isafjord," he said. "What do you think of that, Kark?"

"When a boat is sinking there is no need for anyone to man the steering oar," Kark muttered.

"Aye!" Odd exclaimed. "What you need to know then is how to swim."

"Unless land is so far away that no man, however strong a swimmer, can reach it." Ravn Eriksen looked with distaste at Odd, whom he found too forward. "For then he will merely prolong his death and suffer all the more."

"One must not give up, Uncle." Leif glanced from Odd to Ravn Eriksen. "Is it not one's duty to fight for one's life to the very end?"

"And if one cannot fight?" Ravn Eriksen moved uncomfortably in his chair. "If one has never learned or cared to learn to swing a sword, would one not look foolish doing it?"

"I don't want to fight Egil or anyone." Leif suddenly remembered what Ulv had said. "He is going to marry Ingeborg!"

"Who?" asked his uncle.

"Egil!" Leif spat the name out like a curse.

Ravn Eriksen hid his face. Rather than meet Leif's gaze he looked away to some dark corner of the hall. "And is she willing to marry him?" he whispered.

"I would not think so," Leif said with pride.

"I would not know how to be chieftain, Kark. My back is not straight enough, it bends too easily." Ravn Eriksen was speaking to his servant, but then he turned to his nephew. "I gave you the spear, Leif, and the sword of our ancestors. I will obey your command rather than give mine."

Leif looked so crestfallen that his uncle could not help feeling sorry for him. "I will be your counselor but not your chief," he said.

"Then, if you are my counselor, tell me what I should do?" Leif asked, while Odd smiled sarcastically to himself.

"I would —" Ravn Eriksen began, but at that moment Flose burst into the room.

"They came, the three of them again!" he spluttered, heaving for air for he had run all the way from the pass. "They are up there."

"Who are you talking about?" Leif asked.

"The Gode brothers, Teit, Asgrim, and Kolben." Flose

sank down on the bench by the table. "They want you to come up there and meet them, they say they have a message for you!" He lowered his voice. "They said that if you were not afraid to come they would wait for you."

Leif looked at Odd, then at the still panting Flose. "Sit here for a while until you have caught your breath," he said to the boy. "And then meet me and Odd at our 'hall.'"

"What are you going to do?" Odd asked as soon as they were outside.

"You will take my spear and I will wear the sword. We shall climb to the pass and find out what they want. What else can we do?"

"You never found out what your uncle would do," Odd said.

"No." Leif smiled. "He did not want to be chieftain, so his advice does not matter."

20

Egil Calls a Meeting

THE SWORD that dangled from his belt made Leif feel more foolish than brave. He rested his left hand on the hilt to steady it while he cursed it under his breath at the same time. Odd was carrying the spear and Leif wished they could change weapons. He had left his knife at home. It felt like a part of him when he wore it, but then a knife was not so much a weapon as a tool. A knife, he thought, has a thousand uses and a sword only one.

Leif had tied the dog at home, he did not want it to follow them for the Gode boys might take it as a deliberate insult. But halfway up to the pass the dog came barking, jubilant at having caught up with them. "I am going to let them take you back with them," Leif warned the dog as it jumped between him and Odd, not quite sure which one it wanted to put its paws on.

"They are not hiding, anyway." Flose pointed up to

the place where the three Gode boys were plainly sil-houetted against the sky.

"Teit is the only one of them who has as much brain as he has brawn. Talk to him," Odd advised.

"We used to be friends, I think." Leif wrinkled his brow, for suddenly it occurred to him that he had never before given much thought to who his friends were. True, among the people of Brattahlid and Isafjord there were those whom he liked better than others, but he had not divided his world into friends and foes. "I think I have few friends left at Brattahlid," he said and smiled sadly.

"Kolben is a fool, Asgrim too young to do anything but follow the leader, but Teit Gode is clever and terri-bly proud of kin and family," Odd said earnestly. "Be careful how you treat him, give him more respect than he deserves."

"Are you afraid that I might insult him?" Leif smiled and glanced at Odd.

"Not purposely." Odd paused, thinking about how best to phrase what he was going to say. "You have been brought up to think that Isafjord, and Brattahlid as well, were yours, and that you would be first among the Norsemen of Greenland when you grew up. Teit's father, old Otkel Gode, has been the butt of many jokes and Gunner Ulfson treated him with no respect, so Teit is thin-skinned. The very assurance that you, a chieftain's son, drank with your mother's milk can be an affront to him!" Odd watched Leif's features, for a moment he thought he would become angry, but then Leif laughed and put his hand on Odd's shoulder.

"I was afraid that you would leave with the little people, for then I would have had no one I respect to advise me. But when you do counsel me and give me sound advice, for a moment I felt my cheeks grow hot with anger. Truly we are fools, are we not?"

"I have known no man so wise that he was not part fool, I think wisdom lies in knowing that." Odd grinned. "I think I know Teit Gode's faults because I have a share of them."

As the three boys advanced to the pass their feeling of dignity made them walk straighter, and for the last few yards none of them spoke. Leif and Odd walked side by side, and Flose followed close behind, the iron axe stuck in his belt.

"You wish to speak to me?" Leif halted a little distance from the Gode boys. They too were armed, all carrying spears with pointed heads.

"Egil Sigurdson has sent us to ask you to meet him here the day after tomorrow, when the sun is highest in the sky." As he spoke Teit Gode glanced for a moment up toward the sun.

"Does he want me to come here alone?" Leif asked.

"You can bring whatever two-legged or four-legged dogs you care to." Kolben Gode looked arrogantly at Odd and Flose as he spoke. Odd thought as he looked at the boy, who was both bigger and stronger than he, that here skill would have to win over strength.

"We have no two-legged dogs at Isafjord," Odd replied pleasantly. "At Isafjord no man needs to wag his tail to curry favor."

"You can bring as many or as few as you want," Teit said, giving his brother a glance that was as much as a command to keep quiet. "Egil Sigurdson wishes to discuss with you matters concerning Brattahlid and Isafjord."

"For hundreds of years the people of Brattahlid and Isafjord have lived peacefully, helping each other when there was need for it," Leif said. "And that is the way that we who live at the uttermost end of the world should live. Each year when winter breaks and spring arrives there are fewer Norsemen left to rejoice in the coming of summer. What foolishness it would be to fight each other!"

"We of Brattahlid have no wish to fight you at Isafjord." Teit Gode spoke as if he meant it, but Kolben laughed and shook his spear at Odd, and so belied his brother's words.

"You may bring word to your . . ." Leif almost said "master," but caught himself and said instead, "To Egil Sigurdson, and tell him we will come." Then he turned and, motioning with his right hand to Odd and Flose to follow, walked down toward Isafjord. He would have liked to look back, but he carefully refrained from doing so and thus he did not see little Asgrim Gode, whose spear was much too big for him, stick out his tongue.

"What are you going to do?" Ulv asked. Leif had collected all the youngsters of Isafjord in their "hall."

"I am going to send you to get your cousins, I want us to be as many as we can." Leif looked at Ulv. "They will come?" he asked.

"They are not the kind who will take back a word once given." Ulv looked almost insulted by the doubt cast on his kin.

"I am sure Egil will bring as many as he can, and that means more than we can raise. Do you know if your cousins have any weapons?" Leif asked.

"If they have they will bring them, and I think they can use them as well, the oldest is strong and a full-grown man. He could split Egil in two with his bare hands!" Ulv grew eloquent as he spoke of his kin. "He can carry a sheep under each arm with ease."

"You had better go and get him." Leif laughed. "He alone will be able to rout Egil and his hird."

"I shall bring them tomorrow." Ulv rose and walked with a swagger from the room, pausing at the door to declare, "I hope Egil does not come earlier so that I will miss the fun."

"I hope not either." Odd shook his head. "We shall be in need of your giant kin."

"They were here some years ago, I remember," Leif said. "The oldest went to Unn to ask for Katla in marriage, but being tongue-tied he never spoke a word. But it does not seem to me that he and his brothers are very large."

"They are not." Odd laughed. "But brave enough, and once they have given their word they will stand by it."

"They never asked me to marry them!" Katla, who had been sitting in the back of the room, stood up. "And if they had I wouldn't," she exclaimed, blushing. The boys laughed.

"You could not marry all three of them," Bjarne said, disgusted by the girl's stupidity. He, who was not too clever himself, had the least patience with her.

"But that is what I said — I wouldn't, even if I could," the girl protested, sitting down again.

Leif rose. "We will meet here in the morning and arm ourselves as best we can." The room was cold, for to save wood they had lit no fire. As Leif and Odd stood outside, Leif felt once more like protesting that he did not want to fight, that he was willing to give up everything for peace. But he didn't, for he was no longer sure that it was the truth.

"I think Egil has called the meeting tomorrow not to fight us, but to insult and taunt us," Leif said, looking out over the fjord below. Only a small part of it still had open water; the rest was frozen, the icebergs locked in place until spring. "It is part of a plan of his, an open battle would not please him."

"Still, we shall come prepared!" Odd looked toward the west, where the fjord was broader. "Will any of us be alive come spring?" he asked.

"Who knows?" Leif whispered, suddenly remembering the girl of the little people who had watched Odd in the kayak.

21

A Trap

ULV'S COUSINS did not go back on their word. They came early in the morning. The oldest, Roald, was strong but not such a giant as Ulv had led them to believe. The next, Thor, was just eighteen, and Eyvind, the youngest of the boys, was older than they had expected — the same age as Leif. Two of them were armed with spears, but Eyvind carried merely a stout stick a foot taller than himself which he declared was the weapon he fought best with. Their sister, Ragnhild, had stayed at home to help their mother. She was too young for such sport, Thor declared, and would not have been of any help.

The three brothers were never apart but seemed to form a solid block. When they walked Roald would be first, Thor and Eyvind following side by side, a mere step behind. Obviously Roald was their leader, but it was Thor who spoke for them, never using the word *I* but always saying *we*. Ulv, who was always playing pranks to make the others laugh, never succeeded in making his cousins even smile. Ulv said that they had lived so far apart from all the other Norsemen that they had never learned to laugh. He declared he would teach them the knack of it, even if it took him a year to do so.

When Leif inspected his little army, his hird, he felt a little foolish, as if he had been caught playing a child's game for which he was much too old. Only when he recalled the blood-soaked altar in the church, and the treatment Ulv had received at Egil's hands, did he realize that he was not playing.

That morning when he had told his father where they were going, Leif hoped that by some miracle Magnus Eriksen would change, that he would become the father he wanted, the true ruler of Isafjord. But his father seemed more frightened than ever, fearing for his silver as well as his life. Now, as Leif marched up the path ahead of his little army of boys and half-grown men, he could not help wondering why and how it had come to pass that all the grownups in Greenland had given up hope and yet, at the same time, had hung on to their lives. He explained his perplexity to Odd, who walked beside him.

"My father would have us all stay at Isafjord to protect him and his silver. When I said I had given my word, he whimpered like a frightened child. Why has he become as he is now?"

"There was a great sickness when more than half the Norsemen in Greenland died. It was well before you and I were born." Odd paused, trying to recall exactly when it had taken place. "It must have been when our parents were children. I think that broke the spirit of those who were spared."

Leif nodded, for he had heard of it from his mother, who had lost all her brothers and sisters. The sickness had come in the fall just before the frost. The first who died were buried, but later when the earth had frozen that was not possible. "I know that to him the silver is proof of his own worth and that Norway still exists and that is why I hate that treasure of his."

"Let him keep it." Odd smiled. "It is like a doll to a small child who thinks the world of a rudely carved piece of wood."

"I would take the doll and throw it in the fire," Leif said bitterly, but then he smiled as he recalled something else. "I think my mother and yours as well, from the way they talked, would have liked to put Egil across their knees."

"I wish Egil's mother were still alive." Odd grinned. "For if the old people's tongues don't lie, she was as fierce as a white bear with young."

"They say she treated his father with a stick, and he prayed every evening that God or the devil would take her." Leif laughed. "I saw her once, years ago at Brattahlid, a tall and handsome woman. They say that when

154

he was young Gunner Ulfson used to run in her footsteps like a dog."

"And now he follows her puppy!" Odd shook his head. "Maybe we should have let our mothers go instead of us."

"They would not have gone." Leif glanced toward the pass, which was not far away. "My mother's bravery is all in her mouth, it amounts to little, and you mastered yours as soon as you were weaned."

"That is true enough, my mother could not frighten a hare," Odd agreed. He too kept his eyes on the pass. "Do you think they haven't come, or that they are hiding?"

"I will call a halt when we are near, then you and I will go forward alone." Leif peered up at the sun. "It must be near noon," he said.

"If we have to go up there alone, I shall at least be prepared to use the hare's defense." Odd looked at Leif.

"If we are attacked we shall run for it," Leif agreed. "But not before we are sure; we must not appear cowards either to them or to our own."

"Somehow I do not think they will attack us, this meeting might be a trap." Odd shifted the spear he was carrying from his right shoulder to the left. "But if it is, I cannot yet guess how, or for what purpose."

"It could be merely to give Egil a chance to show himself to his followers," Leif suggested. "A chance to insult us, and so enhance himself."

Odd shook his head. "I think he has other reasons for this meeting besides mere boasting."

"We shall soon know." Leif held up his hand, halted, and turned to speak to his hird. "Odd and I will walk on from here. Be prepared to come to our aid should it be necessary." He then drew his sword from the sheath and, casting a quick glance at Odd to see if he was ready, walked toward the pass.

Just as they came to the point where they could see down as far as Brattahlid they met Egil. He, too, had a sword in his hand, but his was shorter than Leif's. He had but five followers, all armed with spears and one with an iron axe in his belt. With surprise Leif realized that he knew only one of Egil's companions — Skule, the son of his cousin's servants, Thorkil and Astrid. The other four were strangers; two were almost grown men, the others boys of his own age.

Egil lifted his sword as a greeting and then stuck it in his belt, since he had no sheath for it. Leif lifted his, answering the greeting, and then sheathed the weapon. The two boys stepped toward each other, Odd staying with Leif and one of the strangers filling the same office for Egil.

"Welcome." Egil glanced for a moment at Odd, but from then on he kept his gaze on Leif. "I am glad you have come, for it seems to me a shame that those of Brattahlid and Isafjord should not be friends," he said, making a slight nodding movement with his head.

"There are none at Isafjord who would ever wish any-

thing but friendship to all the Norsemen of Greenland."
Leif moved his head as slightly as Egil had bowed his.
"I wish that no Norseman should need to bear arms
against his fellow countrymen."

"Yet you came with your sword drawn." Egil smiled
and his companion, whose two front teeth were miss-
ing, laughed. "Did you fear us?" he asked and then, as
if to answer his own question, added, "If you came here
with thoughts of driving me from Brattahlid, forget any
such intentions. Treat them like dreams that you cannot
recall when you are awake. Once tucked underneath their
bedcovers with their eyes closed all men, even slaves,
can wear a crown."

"Norway may be a country great enough for kings,
but we here in Greenland are too poor for that. I think
a man who would dream of wearing a crown here a
fool." Leif put very little emphasis on the last word; he
did not want to insult Egil.

"Aye, that is true." Egil turned to the man beside him.
"Did I not tell you, Rolf, that Leif of Isafjord is a man
whose tongue is used to speaking the truth?"

The man Egil called Rolf nodded sullenly in agreement and Leif thought, On a wink from his master he
would drive his spear through me, and not think any
more of it than if he had killed a hare.

"I see no reason to call a meeting up here" — Leif
shifted his gaze back to Egil as he spoke — "when we
could meet in each other's halls as friends."

"True. Like a spear rightly cast your words hit their

mark." Nearby were two stones large enough for seats. Egil sat down on one and, pointing to the other, invited Leif to do the same. "Still, I thought it best to meet first on the borders of what we may call our own," Egil said affably.

Leif sat down, wondering what it was all about. He felt certain that some trap had been set, but he could not figure out how or why. Egil talked about his sheep, about what grazing belonged to Brattahlid and what meadows to Isafjord. It was but small talk, and several times Leif caught a smirk on Rolf's face that he did not like, yet one cannot condemn a man for the sake of a smile. Time passed and suddenly it occurred to Leif that this might be the reason for the meeting. He glanced up at the sun; it was lower on the horizon.

He was just about to call Odd to his side when he saw Ulv come running. Sensing that something was wrong, he jumped up just as Rolf cast his spear. It missed, but passed near enough that it would have killed him had he still been sitting on the stone. Leif drew his sword but, seeing Egil's four comrades coming to his aid with spears lifted, he turned and ran. Odd waited until Leif passed him, then he too ran to where the hird stood waiting. Halfway they met Ulv and stopped.

"They have raided Isafjord!" Ulv screamed at them. "Your father's hall is burning!"

22

The Death of Magnus Eriksen

L EIF CURSED the sword, which prevented him from running as fast as he knew he could. Ulv, Odd, and even Flose were ahead of him. The wooden roof of his father's hall was on fire but, to Leif's surprise, no one seemed to be fighting the flames. As he came nearer he could see a lone figure sitting on the ground in front of the building. It was Sven, Odd's father. He was badly wounded, blood flowed from a cut in his head, and Odd was kneeling beside him. Leif looked at his father's old servant and asked, "What happened?" as if he did not already know.

"It was Teit and Atle who were the leaders," Odd said, looking up angrily toward the mountain that hid Brattahlid.

"Your father is in Ravn Eriksen's hall, he is hurt."

"How badly?" Leif asked.

Sven mumbled something he could not understand. "He is dead," Odd whispered.

"No!" Leif shook his head and ran toward his uncle's hall while inside his head the same words echoed over and over, It is not true, it is not true!

But it was true, the ships from Norway had sailed for the last time in Magnus Eriksen's dreams. Now he would never escape the Greenland he had learned to hate, and never tread the halls of the king of Norway. As he lay on the table in the dim light of Ravn Eriksen's hall Magnus appeared more a chieftain than he ever had in life. There was something noble in his features.

"Why did they kill him?" Leif asked his uncle.

"I don't think they meant to." Ravn Eriksen glanced at the body of his brother. "He attacked them when they dug for his silver, and fought like seven devils when they found it. I do not know what made them kill him — anger or fear, or both. I am afraid that Sven is badly hurt too."

"But could they not have . . . just tied him up?" Leif sighed.

Ravn Eriksen shrugged his shoulders. "They could have, and maybe some of them meant to, that we shall never know. All we do know is that someone put a spear through my brother and killed him though he was un-armed." Ravn Eriksen put his hand on his nephew's shoulder. "You must kill Egil, for he is the thorn buried in the flesh and it will not heal until he is gone. Neither

Teit nor Atle matters, and once Egil is no more, those youngsters he brought from Gardar will sail back there."

Leif nodded while he thought, My father was the first to die but he will not be the last, more shall follow, as inevitably as the snow falls in winter.

As if he had guessed his nephew's thought, Ravn Eriksen said, "Try if you can to kill no one else; Egil will go unmourned to his grave, but others might call for revenge."

"Where is Mother?" Leif looked around the room expecting to see her.

"In there." Ravn Eriksen nodded toward one of the smaller rooms that led off the hall. "She was hurt too, but not so badly."

"They would wound an old woman as well?" Leif was truly surprised. "Teit has known her since he was a child."

"Your mother is not wounded, she was just stunned by a blow." Leif's uncle looked down for a moment as if he felt ashamed of being unhurt himself. "It was not Teit or Atle who did it, but someone from Gardar. You can recognize him" — a fleeting smile crossed Ravn Eriksen's face — "by the marks of your mother's nails on his face."

"We have put out the fire," Ulv said. He had entered the room silently and looked intently at the dead body of Magnus Eriksen. "We had to pull down half the roof."

"It must have given them some trouble to light it,"

Leif mumbled, he had not yet understood why they had done it.

"It was meant as a signal to those on the mountain," Ravn Eriksen explained. "To tell them that they had the silver and could let you go."

"The hall does not matter." Leif shrugged his shoulders. "But we have been fools." The boy felt bitterly his own failure. "I did not suspect a trap, if I had my father would not be dead." He turned to his uncle. "You should not have given me the sword or the spear, I am not worthy of them."

"You have not been foolish, it was not your fault." Ravn Eriksen looked kindly at his nephew. "If one had never seen a white bear, how would one know the strength of its claws? We at Isafjord have lived so long at peace with all but nature that we have forgotten what man will do for power over others." Leif's uncle shook his head. "Even now I cannot believe what has happened, it is more as if I were still in the world of dreams struggling to wake up."

"How many were there?" Leif asked.

"Twelve, and not all boys, though those among them who were full grown were young. One I recognized — the child of a cousin of Solveig, Egil's mother. He hails from Gardar, I knew his parents, though little good of them."

"Is my mother's cousin, Gunner Ulfson, part of it?" Leif asked his uncle, looking toward the door. Bjarne had just come in.

"Whether he was or not does not matter," Ravn Eriksen grumbled. "As a child he was always jealous of others, and claiming more than his share."

"My father," Bjarne sniffed, finding it difficult to keep back his tears, "is dead, I think."

"Go!" Ravn Eriksen commanded Leif. "His wife is with your mother, I will tell her. It may not be as bad as that," he said hopefully to Bjarne.

"Oh, it is!" Suddenly tears burst from the boy's eyes and he repeated his words as he followed Leif. "Oh, it is!"

"Where is my mother?" Odd looked up at Leif from the bed where his father was lying. Sven had been carried to the little hut that had been his home all his life, for he had been born there as well.

"She is coming." The room was lit by an oil lamp made of soapstone, but it gave little light and smelled strongly of tallow. "She was with my mother." Leif could hear Bjarne breathing deeply, he was still crying, and all of a sudden the boy realized that he had not yet shed one tear.

"Would it not have been better if she had been here with her husband?" Odd stood up.

"My mother has been hurt," Leif explained. "I am sure if they had known that your father" — in embarrassment the boy lowered his voice — "was dying, my uncle would not have kept her."

"It does not matter," Odd grumbled. Just then his mother entered. Jofrid stood for a moment leaning against the doorpost, as if she did not trust her legs to carry her any farther, then with a strange little cry she threw herself on her husband's lifeless body.

"We must avenge them." Leif spoke the words slowly as if each carried a heavy weight.

"Yes." Odd glanced back at the door of the hut. He felt that he ought to go back inside, yet he did not want to.

"Egil has twice the" — Leif stopped for a moment and then continued with a wry smile — "men that we have."

"Oh, I will kill him!" Odd looked at the sunken roof of the hall nearby, where his father and Leif's had met their deaths.

"What I find so terrible," Leif mumbled, "is the waste of it. I mean" — he turned to his friend — "it was for nothing, for something as worthless as a little chest of silver coins."

"Yes, that is what your father, Magnus Eriksen, died for." Odd kept his voice low as well. "My father was defending yours, the silver did not matter to him."

"So he died for friendship, which makes his death less meaningless than my father's." Leif smiled bitterly. "My father's death was no more noble than his life."

Odd touched Leif's shoulder. "You have not shed a tear yet, and neither have I. My brother is inside crying like a lost child. Whatever happens we shall avenge them, we, the tearless ones." With those words he stretched out his hand and Leif grabbed it.

"If we die," Leif said, "let it be for friendship's sake." And strangely enough, at that moment both boys felt their eyes grow moist.

23

Ingeborg and Bera

"I WANTED to put a cross on the grave of my uncle Olaf, Thorkil made one for me but Egil had it taken away," Ingeborg whispered to Bera. "I went to my father and told him but he said it didn't matter. He said that the crosses were there for the sake of the living and that the dead did not care."

"Maybe he is right." Bera stood up and stretched herself. The two girls shared one of the small rooms of the great hall. It had no opening to the outside and a tallow lamp supplied both light and warmth. "Egil has gone to Isafjord to demand Magnus Eriksen's silver for your father."

Ingeborg hid her face in her hands. "I know, my father claims it is his, but that is not true."

"It is my brother who has put him up to it." Bera cupped her hands round the flame of the lamp, causing strange shadows to dance on the stone walls. "He wants to be ruler of Greenland."

"And what about my cousin Leif?" Ingeborg, who had been lying on the bed the two girls shared, sat up. "Why should he not rule Greenland?"

"If he kills Egil, then he will, and if he doesn't, then Egil will." Bera shrugged.

"And you want your brother to win!" Ingeborg declared.

"No!" Bera shook her head. "He is my brother, I know, but I have never liked him."

"Never?" Ingeborg asked, she had always wanted a brother or a sister.

"Once I had a tame little snow sparrow, it had hurt its wing when I found it. Egil killed it!" Bera glanced for a moment at her companion. "Maybe it would have died anyway, but Egil killed it because I loved that little sparrow."

"Because you loved it?" Ingeborg, who had her favorite goat, understood the girl's feeling for the little bird.

"Egil thinks I should love only him." Bera shook her head. "No, that is wrong, I don't think he cares whether I love or hate him; he is like an eagle that allows no other bird to nest on the same mountaintop. He is like the sun, which shines so strongly that neither stars nor moon can be seen."

"And Leif is the moon or a bright star?" Ingeborg asked. Bera nodded. "He told me but a few days after we had come to Brattahlid that he would kill Leif. He said it differently, he said that Leif would have to die. It was at the time he said that he would marry you."

"And does he tell you everything?" Ingeborg's voice shook with rage.

"He used to." Bera sat down on the bed beside her. "But he doesn't anymore. He knows that he cannot trust me, so he tells me nothing, or only what is of no importance."

"I will never marry him." Ingeborg drew her legs up and, hugging her knees, looked at the lamp, which stood on a little shelf formed by a protruding stone, as if her future were written in its flame. "When you first told me I thought my father would never let him marry me, but now I know that is not true. Egil rules Brattahlid and my father is like an old dog who, being past use, is allowed to live only as long as it pleases his master. But I will not marry him."

"But he wants to marry you." Bera laid her hand on Ingeborg's knee. "You and Leif should flee south to Herjolfness, they say there are still Norsemen living there."

"We couldn't." Ingeborg shook her head. "Leif would not give up his father's farm at Isafjord, and our boat is so leaky that it would sink . . . When I was a child I used to dream that Leif and I lived here, but not in these houses with earth-covered walls like a bear's den. No, I dreamt that we lived in large halls much bigger than the church, and the walls were covered with pictures like the ones my uncle Olaf told about."

"Like the hall of the kings of Norway?" Bera smiled as she spoke. "I had no dreams like that. A nightmare used to visit me; in my dreams an eagle, much larger than any I had ever seen, would swoop down upon me and carry me away high up in the sky."

"And then what happened?"

"Oh." Bera laughed. "It would drop me and I would fall."

"And then?" Ingeborg looked eagerly at Bera.

"Then I would wake up," she answered.

"And so would everybody else in the house," a deeper voice said. Egil was standing in the doorway. "For every time she would scream as loud as a lost soul at midnight."

"Is it usual among you and yours to steal into each other's rooms without knocking on the door?" Ingeborg asked, wondering at the same time how long Egil had stood there and how much he had heard.

"We had only one room in that hut we called our hall, and the only one that knocked on our door was the wind when it came sweeping down from the ice." Egil was surprised, for in truth he had not even thought of knocking at the door before opening it. "Have you been telling secrets that were not for my ears?" he asked his sister.

"Every word we have said was meant for you to hear."

Bera bent her head. "But we are not going to look in corners or under beds to make sure that you are not listening."

"You need not worry, your secrets are of no more interest to me than the twittering of birds." Egil lied, for he cared passionately what others thought of him. "I came to tell you that your cousin Magnus Eriksen was slain."

"And my cousin Leif?" Ingeborg pressed herself up against the corner of the wall as if she wanted to get as far away as possible from Egil.

"Nothing has happened to him, not yet." Egil grinned. "If he is sensible he will live, and if he is not . . ." The boy clicked his tongue and somehow in the still room the noise was meaningful.

"Did you have to kill him?" Gunner Ulfson handled the little wooden chest carefully. He had opened its lid several times, there were nearly two handfuls of silver coins inside. "He was a cousin of my wife's," he added, as if that were of importance now.

"He would not give it up." Egil looked with disgust at the older man, who kept fondling the treasure chest like a woman with a newborn child.

"Aye." Gunner Ulfson nodded, he understood that, he too would rather die than give up his silver. "Could you not have tied him up?" The question was the same that Leif had asked his uncle.

"One of my men was a little too eager." Egil shrugged his shoulders. "I have already said I was sorry to Ingeborg."

"Who was it that killed him?" Gunner Ulfson asked, taking his eyes off the chest in his lap for a moment.

"I am not sure whether it was Atle or Teit." Egil yawned to show how little he cared and sat down.

"I would not like it to be Atle. He is my servant's child and not a freeborn man." Gunner wrinkled his brow in perplexity; he was proud of his lineage and knew that Magnus Eriksen had been so too.

"Earl Hakon, so we are told, was killed by his slave," Egil said, scratching his head. "But that was long ago, we are all freeborn men today."

"Free to murder!" Ingeborg stood in the doorway, Bera was beside her.

"Now, Ingeborg." Gunner Ulfson looked unhappily at his daughter.

"It was all a mistake, I am sure," he said lamely, wishing that everyone would leave him alone so that he could add Magnus Eriksen's silver to his own treasure.

"A mistake to kill your own kin!" Ingeborg's eyes flashed in anger. "Earl Hakon was not the last man to be killed by a slave." She spluttered as she turned and left the hall.

"She is young." Gunner Ulfson looked apologetically at Egil. "She will forget it," he added.

"It does not matter." Egil drew his dagger from his belt and started to clean his fingernails. "One man will rule in Greenland, and those who do not understand that will be taught to." The boy glanced at his hand and stuck the dagger back in his belt. The knife had once belonged to Gunner Ulfson.

"Ingeborg is a sensible girl." Her father nodded his head several times, but did not look at Egil and did not see his expression of contempt.

24

Geir from Gardar

I WOULD rather you had not killed him, but that you killed his servant was well done." Egil looked at Teit and Atle, whom he had made his officers; it was Teit who had been in command of the band that had raided Isafjord and murdered Magnus Eriksen.

"It was Geir from Gardar who did it. I think he was scared." Teit shrugged his shoulders. "It was lucky that his wife, Greta, was not killed as well, Geir got his cheeks clawed bloody by her."

"Serves him right." Egil smiled. "You will have to keep better command over your men."

"Magnus Eriksen fought like a bear," Atle said, coming to Teit's defense.

"And so you skinned him." Egil laughed and the two boys, who had not been sure how they stood with their leader, joined him. "We need to slaughter two sheep, I do not want those who came from Gardar to complain that their bellies grumble."

"I will slaughter the sheep, my brother Skule will help me," Atle offered.

"Take three men with you. Leif Magnusson has sheep grazing on his southern meadow by the lake, he won't mind our borrowing them." Egil looked around the small hut, which had belonged to Olaf Ulfson and which he had made his own. "We can always tell him that we used them for a wake for his father."

"Yes!" Atle jumped up, eager to obey.

"Wait." Egil held up a restraining hand. "Make it three sheep. Magnus Eriksen was a great chieftain, so it would not be honorable to skimp at his funeral feast."

"You will anger Leif!" Teit said as soon as Atle had gone.

"More for killing three sheep than for killing his father?" Egil looked quizzically at the boy.

"No, I suppose it does not matter now." Closing his eyes, Teit could still see the dying Magnus on the floor of his hall. "But you mock Leif by stealing his sheep."

"That is what I want." Egil, who had been sitting on the bed where he slept at night, leaned back against the wall while he scrutinized the boy who stood uncomfortably twisting his hands. "Who is to rule Greenland must be decided before the midwinter feast. I want to make him desperate enough to do something foolish. Besides, he has more sheep than we."

"I have known Leif for a long time, though it cannot be said that we have been friends," Teit grumbled.

"It is either him or me." Egil smiled again. "But do you think you can become friends with Leif now? Remember, you were in command when his father was killed."

"No." Teit looked uncomfortably down at the floor.

"You have chosen." Egil's smile became a grin. "Leif will either be master of Brattahlid instead of me, or dead. If he is killed, someone else must have the farm at Isafjord." The expression on Egil's face changed as he spoke these last words, making quite obvious to whom he was offering it.

"I have chosen." Teit nodded while he thought, If I get the farm at Isafjord, the name Gode will mean something in Greenland again.

Egil looked earnestly at Teit. "We are blood brothers now. The blood of Magnus Eriksen binds us more securely than if we had mixed our own."

"You are our chieftain," Teit agreed, but so reluctantly that Egil scowled.

"Go and find me Geir from Gardar." The smile returned to Egil's face, making it seem more cruel. "It is a fine-sounding name, is he well connected there?"

"In Gardar?" Teit was a little taken aback by the question, until he remembered that Egil had been born and brought up at the bottom of the fjord in one of the loneliest spots in Greenland. "He is as well born as any in Gardar, I think he can even claim some kinship with Leif's mother, Greta Helgasdaughter."

"That is good, for that makes the killing a family affair. Go and fetch him."

As soon as Teit had gone Egil got up. Fetching a bone comb, he combed his hair, then he put Gunner Ulfson's sword beside him on the bed and sat down again to wait for the arrival of Geir from Gardar.

Geir was not a boy, nineteen summers had gone by since he was born. He was well built, but not tall. His right cheek was marked by three long streaks of dried blood. Egil rose as he entered and greeted him warmly, then sat down again upon the bed, inviting Geir to make use of the small wooden stool.

"I want to ask your advice," Egil began, watching the expression on the young man's face, "about what further to do in the matter of Isafjord."

"I did not mean to kill him," Geir interrupted. "Had he not attacked me I would have let him be."

Egil smiled. "It was a mistake. But do you think Leif will be satisfied if we tell him that?"

"Won't he have to be?" Geir, who had feared he was going to be reproved more severely for his deed, smiled slyly. "We have twice the men that he has."

"Oh, that is true." Egil nodded as if he had never had that thought himself. "Still, one would like to be at peace with whoever rules Isafjord. I am afraid that there is blood spilled in this matter, and blood calls for vengeance in blood."

Geir looked earnestly at Egil. "Leif will not forgive his father's murder."

"No, he will not think it a mistake." The boy looked at the young man opposite him, like a cat at a mouse. "He will demand your life, you can be sure of that!"

"Oh, I can protect myself," Geir replied with a grin. "He is, after all" — the young man was going to say "just a boy," but realizing that Egil and Leif must be the same age he said instead — "unskilled in the use of weapons."

"That is true," Egil agreed. "What I would like to see is someone who is a friend to Brattahlid sitting in the chieftain's seat at Isafjord."

Geir from Gardar, who was just about clever enough to seek shelter if it rained, said, "I think it is going to be hard to make a friend of Leif now," showing that he had not grasped Egil's hint.

"It would indeed." Egil sighed; he suffered fools badly though he never objected to using them. "That is why I thought that if someone whom I trusted as my friend lived at Isafjord, instead of Leif, we would all be better off." As Geir frowned, Egil added in a tone more irritated than generous, "Someone like yourself."

"Oh, I could easily kill him. I am both stronger and older than he is." Geir from Gardar had finally understood Egil and added naively, "I would like to be chieftain of Isafjord."

"Do not tell anyone what has been said here!" Egil looked distastefully at the young man. "It could be misunderstood."

"Oh, I can keep my mouth shut." Geir looked around the room as if to make certain that no one had been listening.

"I am sure of that." Egil answered, smiling in spite of himself. "I have been told that you are related to Leif's mother. Is that true?"

"She is my father's cousin." Geir from Gardar was already sitting in the chieftain's chair at Isafjord, home in Gardar there were two older brothers.

"Then if Leif should die, you are his nearest kin and could lay claim to the farm."

"That I could." Geir frowned and added truculently, "And I would too." He somehow felt that in killing Leif he would only be vindicating an old right out of which he had been cheated.

"We shall see." Egil rose and Geir got up too. "The final battle between Brattahlid and Isafjord will take place next full moon, I shall decide the day in good time." Egil put his hand on Geir's shoulder. "But Leif is yours, I shall tell the others not to touch him. Since you are to receive the prize, it is best you pluck it. Do not underestimate Leif, he may not be skilled with weapons but he is no fool."

Geir did not answer but merely growled contemptuously as he took his leave. He has the courage of a dog, Egil thought, and then smiled. It had suddenly occurred to him how fortunate he would be if Leif, before he died, could have the luck to wound Geir from Gardar beyond healing.

25

Leif's Decision

LEIF WAS sitting alone in the abandoned hut that the children called their "hall." The last family to live there had perished during that winter when so many of the Norsemen in Greenland had died. The timbers that held up the roof were rotten; through a hole a beam of sunshine shot downward to illuminate the earthen floor. That morning Leif had buried his father and his servant Sven. Magnus Eriksen and Odd's father had been laid in the same grave, master and servant becoming one. The decay of the building, which the rain and wind had worn and torn for several hundred years, depressed the boy. As he had entered, a feeling of melancholy engulfed him. Here they had held counsel when they were children playing Vikings and planned raids upon nonexistent enemies. In his eyes then, Leif's hall had been as glorious a construction as any that ever housed a king of Norway.

Lost in his dreams of times past, he did not notice

Odd until the boy spoke, asking him where Ulv's cousins were. For a moment Leif did not understand so plain a question; it was as if his soul had gone on a journey and only with the greatest difficulty could he call it back. "I have sent them to the upper pastures," he finally said, "to bring down what sheep we have there."

"That was wise, they were too near Brattahlid, we do not need to provide a larder for Egil," Odd said approvingly as he sat down opposite him.

"Do you know that the man who killed my father and yours was my mother's kin?" Leif drew some meaningless figures in the dust on the table. "She recognized him, his name is Geir."

"Geir." Odd tasted the name and then made a face as if he did not find it to his liking. "He killed them because that was the easiest."

"My uncle Ravn once told me that in the time of the Vikings in Norway, and I think in Iceland too, there were Norsemen who killed for the love of it. They were called Berserks."

"And do you think that Geir is a Berserk?" Odd asked.

"Yes." Leif glanced at his friend. "You and I would do anything to avoid killing someone. But Geir would not, I think he enjoyed it. My father and yours were troublesome to him, so they had to die. That is the way a Berserk acts."

"That is why Egil got him from Gardar, to swing his sword for him," Odd agreed. "Then if it comes to battle we must attack him first, once he is out of the way Egil may lose his courage."

"It is me he will kill." Leif smiled as he contemplated his own death. "So long as I live Egil will have no right to Brattahlid. Even if he should kill Gunner Ulfson and force my cousin to marry him, he will not sit securely in his chieftain's seat."

"Ingeborg will never marry him!" Odd exclaimed.

"No," Leif agreed. "But her father might force her."

"Gunner Ulfson is a fool!" Odd dismissed the master of Brattahlid with contempt.

"I think we should free her and bring her to Isafjord." Leif looked away, wondering if what he was about to propose was wise. "If we have Ingeborg the right to Brattahlid is taken from Egil."

"What if she does not want to come?" Odd asked.

"Then . . ." Leif recalled his cousin's features as vividly as if she were standing in front of him. "She will come," he continued. "I am certain of that."

"You should marry her," Odd argued. "Then there will be no doubt about your rights."

"The last people married in Greenland were married by Olaf Ulfson. He is dead, he knew what was written in the book of the priest, now no one knows the words that bind a man and a woman together."

"You spoke over your father, and mine too, saying words that will make them rest in their graves." Suddenly Odd smiled. "I will be priest and marry you, it will be as good as if it had been done by the bishop of Gardar, or all the monks who ever lived at Ketilsfjord."

"Be it so." Leif grasped Odd's hand. "If she is willing you shall play the priest, but not before Egil has gone from Brattahlid and we have cleaned the altar in the church there."

"If Brattahlid is Ingeborg's and Isafjord is yours, then if we lose you we lose it all." Odd looked straight at Leif. "Maybe it would be better that I should lead those who will bring back your bride."

"No." Leif shook his head. "Though there are those who may even be right" — here Leif smiled — "I will fight Egil or die in the attempt, for if I don't —" Leif paused for a moment and sighed. "I might become like my father, a man of no account." The boy lowered his voice so that Odd could hardly hear as he whispered, "Of no account even to himself."

"But then at least," Odd said, giving up his point, "let me, Ulv, or his cousins be beside you to ward off that Berserk of Egil's."

"Oh, I leave him willingly to the first man who can kill him." Leif grinned. "What about Ulv's cousin Roald? I think him fierce enough to earn the title of Berserk."

"Without those three we would stand little chance against Egil's hird." Odd smiled. "Do you know that my brother has visited their farm more than once? It is their sister, Ragnhild, who has made him wander so far."

"What is she like?" Leif asked, without real interest.

He tried to conjure another picture of his cousin Inge-borg in his mind, but to his surprise it was Egil's sister, Bera, he saw. This disturbed him so much that he did not listen to what Odd was saying. "Do you believe in the power of dreams and omens?" he asked.

"Most people do." Odd looked around the hall as if he expected something supernatural to appear. "But I am not sure it is not foolish. Your father dreamt often enough that the ships of the king of Norway would come, but no ship ever came."

"That is true." Leif nodded. "But right now, for no reason at all, like a shadow cast upon the ground from a cloudless sky, I feel that I shall never wed Inge-borg."

Odd was about to reply when Ulv and his three cous-ins entered, out of breath. "Egil's men have killed three of our ewes, they had just slaughtered them when we came upon them." Ulv looked proudly from Leif to Odd. "They were five and we were four, but we beat them and wounded one of them."

"Who were they?" Leif asked.

"Atle, Skule, Kolben, and Asgrim; Atle was the leader." Ulv had gotten his breath back again.

"I thought you said there were five," Odd said.

"There were! But the fifth was someone we did not know, I think he had come from Gardar."

"A man or a boy?" Leif asked.

"A boy," Ulv replied.

184

"And whom did you wound?" Odd asked. The victory had not been great, since two of the four from Isafjord were grown men.

"Asgrim Gode," Ulv admitted shamefacedly. Knowing there was little glory in the deed he added, "I do not think he was badly wounded."

"This must be little Asgrim's twelfth summer." Leif shook his head, wishing passionately that the boy had not been hurt.

"It is well that they at Brattahlid have been taught that they cannot steal our sheep unpunished," Odd interrupted hastily as he saw the discouragement all too apparent on Ulv's and his cousins' faces.

"Let us attack Brattahlid at sunrise the day after tomorrow." It was a sudden decision on Leif's part, but as he spoke he realized that it was the right one. "If we wait we shall surely be defeated. In the game of chess you lose if you do not attack."

"Only a game, not your life." Odd wrinkled his brow. "Egil has more men than we have."

"Yes, and the longer we wait the more they will be. Soon the ice on the fjord will be thick enough to make the passage to Gardar secure, maybe Egil will find more friends to come to his aid."

"When eagles fight the ravens grow fat." Ulv quoted the proverb.

"Neither Egil nor I is an eagle," Leif said, smiling, "nor are we ravens." Then turning to Odd he continued his argument. "We shall attack the main hall from two directions."

"We are not enough to split ourselves into two groups," Odd objected.

"One group will attack from the beach, where they will have hidden, I hope unnoticed by Egil's guards; you shall lead them, Odd. The other will approach from the hill in full view of any sentries who might be posted. Egil will think we are fewer than we are, and he will leave his hall to fight in the open."

"Each of us will have to fight for two," Odd suggested cautiously.

"Why don't you run to the little people?" Odd's brother had entered the hall unseen by the others. "He has a girl there!" Bjarne looked triumphantly around the room. "She is as fat and ugly as a seal," he announced, and when Flose and Eyvind, the youngest of Ulv's cousins, grinned, he added, "And she smells like one, too."

"If you were not my brother —" Odd clenched his hands in fury, but thought better of it and merely shrugged his shoulders.

"Of those who have joined Egil from Gardar there is one man who is particularly fierce, he is called Geir." Leif looked at Roald. "He is as dangerous as a white bear, whether he smells like one we had better ask Bjarne who seems to have so keen a nose."

"Send my brother in to sniff at him, as one sets a dog on a bear," Odd said with a laugh.

"Let me at him!" Roald shook his head like a ram ready to butt. "I will finish him off and skin him as well."

"You are more than welcome to him," Odd replied, "but he will prove more difficult than little Asgrim Gode."

26

Ingeborg and Egil

WHAT WAS my mother like?" Ingeborg looked at Astrid, she had asked the question before and knew that the answer the servant woman gave would not satisfy her.

"She was beautiful," the woman answered, with as much expression as if she had commented on the weather.

"I know, that is what my father answers, too, when I ask him. I am sure that she was beautiful, but was she —" Ingeborg searched in her mind for the right word, but it escaped her and instead of what she wanted to say she asked, "Was she good?"

The question was so strange that Astrid paused to think it over, for she had never thought before whether those who commanded her were good. "They all wanted her," she finally said. "All the men, and it is very hard to be good then."

Ingeborg smiled. Astrid had never been beautiful and maybe she was right that goodness and beauty seldom go together. "How is my father this morning?" she asked. "He complained last night that he was not well."

"It is neither sickness nor age, it is Egil who is the cause of it all." Astrid looked around the small room where the food at Brattahlid was prepared as if she expected to find Egil lurking in a corner. "He should send that boy and his father back to the ice-covered land he came from. He is like his mother and she was bad." Astrid shook her head in dismay. "Bad, bad, bad."

"And she was beautiful too." Ingeborg turned to go, she had often heard about Egil and Bera's mother.

"No, she wasn't," Astrid called after her. "She was ugly, ugly!"

I wonder, thought Ingeborg as she entered the main hall, if that is true. She knew that her father was supposed to have been in love with Solveig. Seeing him seated by the table she approached, wishing to ask him what Egil's mother had been like. But the question died on her lips at the sight of his face, which was pale like the snow that covered the ground outside. "Don't sit here, the hall is cold, Father. Come into my room where it is warm," she said, laying her hand on his shoulder.

Gunner Ulfson turned his head slowly, as if it were difficult and painful to do so, and looked at his daughter. "I had a dream last night," he whispered.

"Yes, Father." Ingeborg sat down on the bench near

him, she wanted to take his hand but he pushed hers away.

"Magnus came." Gunner Ulfson nodded his head as if he were agreeing with what he said. "He wanted his silver back."

"Did you give it back to him?" Ingeborg asked, for the moment almost forgetting that this was a dream and that Magnus Eriksen was dead.

"I promised I would give it to Leif." Gunner Ulfson looked beseechingly at his daughter. "But he doesn't care for silver, does he?" he asked.

"If you promised in your dream to give it to Leif, don't you think you should do so?" Ingeborg smiled as you smile at a child you want to coax into being good.

"You know him, next time he comes tell him he can have something else." Gunner Ulfson paused. "Tell him he can have the boat instead," he said, smiling cunningly.

"I will." Ingeborg nodded, knowing perfectly well that Egil would never give up the boat and that Leif could only enter Brattahlid at the cost of his life. "Come and rest in my room, we have a lamp burning there and it is warm." Gently she guided her father to the little room she shared with Egil's sister, and he lay down on her bed willingly. She covered him and stayed until he had fallen asleep, then she went in search of Bera.

"I want you to stay and take care of my father, I am going to Isafjord to be with Leif," Ingeborg not so much asked as commanded Bera, whom she had found talking to Atle.

"I cannot protect your father." Bera shook her head.

"Where is he now?" she asked.

"I put him in our bed, he was sitting in the hall with his face as pale as snow." Ingeborg's brow was furrowed. "Maybe you should come with me to Isafjord, and we will take my father too."

"No." Bera looked curiously at Ingeborg. "It would not do for me to go." She is not jealous, she thought. "I will protect your father as well as I can here, but I have no power over Egil even though he is my brother."

"I hate him!" Ingeborg looked toward the hall just at the moment when Egil came out. He looked up at the sky as if he were judging what weather it held; then, seeing the two girls, he walked down to them. "I won't talk to him," Ingeborg said, stamping her foot, which made Bera smile.

"When shall we hold our wedding?" Egil grinned at Ingeborg, who moved back and hid behind Bera. "At the midwinter feast, when the gods and the sky are closest to man?" Egil spied Atle and called him. The boy came, but walking, not running, and for a moment Egil's eyes narrowed. "How is Asgrim Gode?" he asked.

"There is fever in his wound, his brothers are with him." Atle glanced at Ingeborg and Bera.

"We shall make them pay for that wound," Egil promised.

"But why did we have to rob Leif of his sheep?" Ingeborg had forgotten her threat. "We of Brattahlid have never stooped to stealing," she said disdainfully.

"And we of Brattahlid still do not steal, we merely demand our rights." Egil emphasized the last word.

I wonder if he believes it, Bera thought as she heard Ingeborg ask what rights he was talking about.

"The rights of chieftainship." Egil glanced for a moment at Atle. "Why do you think that all has gone as it has here in Greenland? Why are the halls of the Norsemen empty and their graveyards full?"

"Because sickness has come. That is the reason," Ingeborg snorted angrily. "And if anybody other than my father is to be chieftain of Brattahlid, it is my cousin Leif."

"Leif . . . the Unlucky." Egil tasted the title that he had given Leif Magnusson, and finding it to his liking he repeated it. "Leif the Unlucky."

"Is there anything you wished me for?" Atle interrupted. "Otherwise it is time to bring the goats down and have them milked."

"I want you to keep a watch on Ingeborg," Egil replied with a smile, "and on my sister as well. I think Leif from Isafjord might want to steal them from us. We would not want that, would we?"

"I am not in danger from anyone at Isafjord, I need no one to guard me." Ingeborg gave a contemptuous toss of her head and was about to leave when Egil grasped her by the shoulders and held her. She could feel the strength of his hands through her clothes.

"You will learn to obey," he snarled, and then when he saw fear in the girl's face he let her go.

27

The Battle!

Wᴇ ꜱʜᴀʟʟ wait here until you are safely hidden down by the beach. Then, when the first rays of the sun paint the snow on the mountain red, we shall march down, not hiding our approach." Leif looked around his little flock; his uncle Ravn had insisted on joining them, he and his servant, Kark, stood a little apart. "You, Odd, with Roald, Thor, and Eyvind shall attack them from the rear. I think, if I know Egil, he will not be near the fighting. He prefers others to do the killing for him, so your coming from the beach may catch him unawares."

"If we do, I shall send my spear through him," Odd said, lifting his spear a little.

"And I shall go after Geir." Roald the silent growled like a bear.

"Catch Egil first, once he is gone the Berserk from Gardar will prove a sheep," Leif said jokingly, though he was far from sure. Then he shook the hands of Odd and Ulv's cousins, and they all watched them disappear in the gloom. The four were not following the usual path to Brattahlid but were traveling a longer route that they hoped would leave them unseen.

"When I was a youngster," Ravn Eriksen said, smiling, "my father liked to tell what he remembered of the old tales. A favorite of his was Egil the Bald's saga. My brother, your father, liked to hear them, but I was not bloodthirsty enough to care for them. No man ever seemed to die in bed in those stories and now, to prove them more right than I thought, poor Magnus is already slain and I am walking, or will be, toward the same fate."

Leif, who had been watching for the slightest pink on the mountains, said a little impatiently, "Uncle, I asked you to stay at home, I did not beg you to come."

"Oh, I know it is all my own making, and I will swing my cudgel with the rest of you." Ravn Eriksen sighed. "But if I should die and Kark live, be good to him." For a moment the brother of the dead chieftain of Isafjord looked at his servant and then whispered, "He has been my friend all my life. I gave him the name Kark as a joke. Kark was the slave who betrayed Earl Hakon, but he would never betray me."

"I shall take good care of him," Leif promised, secretly adding, "if I should live to do so."

"There was one part of the story of Egil the Bald that

I liked but my brother didn't. When he grew old and lived to be more than eighty, he got the idea of going to the Tinge, where all the wisest and most powerful men of Iceland meet to decide law and justice, and there throwing amongst them his whole fortune, which he kept in silver coins. He wanted to see them fight over the metal, like so many ravens over a dead sheep." Ravn Eriksen laughed loudly. "It was a great idea, but the husband of his granddaughter, with whom he lived, would not let him go to the Tinge that year."

"I think Egil the Bald was right." Leif glanced at Ulv, who stood listening nearby. "Don't you?" he asked.

Ulv laughed. "I think it would have been fun to see all the great men down on the ground scrabbling for the coins," he said.

"Egil the Bald would never have seen it" — Ravn had stopped laughing — "for he was blind by then, that is why he could be kept from attending the Tinge. He had his revenge on his grandchildren, he threw all his treasure in a boghole before he died and no one has ever found it."

"When was the last time that the Tinge was held here?" Leif asked. The mountaintop was growing red.

"Long before my grandfather's time," Ravn Eriksen said. "By then it was already a custom of the past. The bishop held his court in Gardar and he thought it a heathen custom."

"It was a great thing that men could come together to solve their own affairs like that," Leif said, thinking that if such meetings were still held he could have brought his feud with Egil and had him declared an outlaw for the murder of his father.

"Justice was not always found there," Ravn Eriksen said. "Often at the Tinge the strongest, most powerful man was also declared the righteous one, even though he came there with bloodstained hands."

"The mountaintop is turning red, Leif." Katla, Unn the Wise's daughter, interrupted them. She held in her hand a cudgel and in her belt was a bone knife with a sharp point.

"Let us go." Leif drew his sword from its sheath and pointed it down the mountain toward Brattahlid.

Leif wished that Odd were walking next to him instead of Ulv, but Odd had been the natural choice to lead the party that was to attack Egil from the beach. Ulv's cousins were brave enough, and Roald might even be a match for Geir from Gardar, but none of them could be trusted to lead. When they were halfway down the mountain Leif saw someone running to the hall, and he guessed it was the guard who kept watch. He smiled to himself and thought, Egil will think we are so few that we have not come to fight but to commit self-slaughter.

Seven they were: two old men, one girl, and four boys who could not grow enough hair among them to make one decent beard. Leif did not think that his uncle Ravn would be much help, nor Kark for that matter, but they added to the group, making it seem more formidable. He tried to count how many were on Egil's side. There were the two Gode brothers, Teit and Kolben; the third, Asgrim, was wounded and only a child. Then there were Skule and Atle and their sister, Gunhild; she would not fight and Atle, he could not help feeling, might be won over to his side. But three or four had come from Gardar, and there were several farms farther down the fjord where there were young people who might have joined him. Still, once it came to a fight could they be trusted?

We are so few Norsemen left in Greenland, Leif thought, and now we march to slaughter each other.

"Halt!" Teit shouted, standing in front of the men and boys from Brattahlid. "What do you want?"

"I would speak with your chief, where is Egil?" Leif shouted back, quickly counting how many they were. Twelve — only one more than they were once the group from the beach had attacked, but quite a few were older and some had swords, and then there was Egil, who would make thirteen.

"You can say what you want to me, Leif." Teit Gode smiled disdainfully. "Have you come to beg my pardon for having wounded my brother?"

"Thieves who come to steal sheep risk being sheared when caught. Though it is a shame that poor Asgrim should get hurt on Egil's errand." From where he stood, Leif could see the heads of Odd and Ulv's cousins peeking above the nearby brink; it looked as though they hâd been executed and the heads laid out in a row. The sight made Leif smile.

"It was very courageous to fight a child." Leif's smile had angered Teit Gode. "But now there are no small boys to frighten."

"Whoever sent your little brother on a man's errand was not very kind, Teit." Leif glanced for a moment toward Geir from Gardar, who had a drawn sword in his hand. "Better that he had played at being a warrior than tried to be one."

"Watch out, Leif!" Ulv shouted, and to Leif's surprise a spear flew by that had been cast from behind. He turned. Three boys were attacking them from the rear. A shout, or roar, like that of a white bear made him turn back. Geir from Gardar was coming toward him swinging his sword as if it were a scythe.

For the shortest of moments fear and surprise lamed him, then he shouted as loud as he could, "Follow me!" and advanced to meet the wild Berserk. When the two swords met in the air Leif felt his arm stunned and for a moment feared that he would lose his weapon. But as Geir drew back to raise his sword for a second blow Ulv cast his spear and hit the Berserk on the left shoulder. Geir screamed in pain and anger and turned to attack Ulv, who stood defenseless. This gave Leif his chance.

Taking the sword in both hands, he swung it hard. The blade bit into Geir's neck so that blood spurted high from the wound.

All was now confusion and screams of pain and fear. Leif saw his uncle's servant, Kark, fight with Kolben Gode, but Ravn Eriksen could not be seen anywhere. Flose was fighting Atle, who was by far the stronger of the two. He held Flose down on the ground, a knife in his hand. "Let him be!" Leif screamed, prepared to kill Atle if he did not obey. The boy looked at Leif and his bloody sword, then let go of Ulv's brother and rose slowly. Leif lowered his sword and said, "We have known each other since we first could stumble on our legs, why have you turned against me?" When the boy did not answer, Leif asked, "Will you serve me now?"

"I will," Atle mumbled and looked around him, "and so will my brother, Skule."

"Where is Egil?" Leif asked. He could hear Odd shouting and Roald roaring. Somewhere in the distance the battle was still going on. "He was in the hall with Ingeborg and his sister," Atle said, nodding toward the main building. "Come!" Leif shouted, and ran toward the hall, Atle and Flose following him.

"You can have the boat, Leif!" Gunner Ulfson said, stepping out from among the shadows of the otherwise empty hall. "The boat is all yours. It is a very good boat."

"Where is Ingeborg?" Leif looked with disgust at the master of Brattahlid.

"I didn't — I didn't mean any harm." Gunner Ulfson stuttered as he saw that the sword in Leif's hand was bloody.

"Where is Egil?" Leif screamed.

"I don't know, I don't know . . ." Gunner Ulfson shook his head. "They were here only a short while ago."

As Leif ran from the hall he heard the master of Brattahlid say once more, "You can have the boat, Leif!"

28

The Death of Egil

W HERE IS Ingeborg?" Leif asked, he had found
Odd who was unhurt.

"She is . . ." The boy hesitated, not knowing if he
should tell the truth, but then he blurted out, "She is
dead, Leif."

"Why?" Leif looked incredulously at Odd and repeated his question. "Why?"

"Egil was dragging both his sister and Ingeborg with
him when Roald cast his spear. It missed Egil." Odd
looked away and said no more.

"The fool!" Leif roared and raised his sword as if he
were willing at that moment to slay Ulv's cousin.

"His brothers are with him, they are trying to keep
him from killing himself." Odd looked earnestly at Leif.
"Your uncle Ravn is dead too, he was killed by Teit
Gode. But you need not avenge him, Roald has already
done that for you."

"I am sorry . . ." Leif lowered his sword. "Poor Ingeborg. And where is Bera, does Egil hold her still?"

"Yes, I saw him running toward the beach pulling her along, much against her will."

"Then come follow me!" Leif shouted while he thought, Egil killed Ingeborg, he is to blame for everything. Catching sight of someone on the fjord he shouted as loud as he could, "I will kill you, Egil!"

"He has Bera with him still," Odd declared as the boys halted by the beach.

"Surely he would not harm his own sister?" Leif glared at his enemy, who was facing him a stone's throw away out upon the ice.

"He would kill her and think no more of it than the falcon when it kills a sparrow." It was Atle who spoke, now full of hate for Egil. "He would do anything" — he lowered his voice to a whisper — "anything at all."

"That was his strength." Leif peered at the boy out on the ice as if he were seeing him for the first time.

"And that was his weakness as well," Odd added, "for it made his followers fear him. Those without honor or conscience always end pierced by their own swords."

"That has not happened yet." Leif glanced about him. "You, Odd, go as far as the end of the beach," he commanded. "And you, Atle and Flose, over to that big boulder. Then when I advance, you three advance as well. In this way we shall attack Egil from three sides, making it difficult for him to escape."

Leif waited until he saw that the other boys had reached their positions, then with drawn sword he stepped out upon the ice of the fjord. There was a thin layer of snow on top, and Leif walked slowly following the tracks made by Egil and Bera. When he came within earshot he halted and shouted, "Let your sister go, Egil, and I will meet you alone."

"I am alone, Leif!" Egil shouted back. "But you are not, call off your dogs!"

"One of them used to be yours." Leif grinned. "Why don't you try to make him wag his tail now?"

"That cur is of no use, he should have been drowned when he was a pup." Egil spat in Atle's direction, then lifted his sword as if he were going to pierce Bera with it.

"She is your sister!" Leif shouted, making a sign to the others that they should approach no nearer. "The same mother carried you."

"And what does that matter?" Egil laughed. "She hates me more than anyone else in all of Greenland. Why should she live if I must die?" He screamed as he pressed down the sword, but its blade missed the girl, who threw herself forward with such force that Egil lost his hold on her. Bera crawled away as fast as she could while Leif and the other boys hurried to her aid. Egil lifted his sword once more, but hesitated and then turned and ran farther out upon the ice of the fjord.

"Let him be!" Bera begged, gripping Leif around the legs. "Let him be!"

"Why should I? He would have killed you!" Leif freed himself from the girl's hold.

"He might take your life!" the girl moaned, but Leif did not hear her as he ran in pursuit of Egil.

The song of the ice beneath his pounding feet suddenly changed its tune and Leif slackened his pace. The ice is growing thinner, he thought, and a fear far more powerful than his wish for revenge made him halt. Ahead of him Egil was still fleeing when suddenly, a spear's length away from an imprisoned iceberg, he disappeared. Twice he screamed as he tried to climb back onto the ice, but it broke under his weight and then all was still.

As Leif crossed himself he heard a low moaning noise, as if nature were sighing over the fate of Egil. He shivered, turned, and ran as fast as he could back toward land. That is the noise the ice makes when it splits and breaks, he thought, expecting any moment to share Egil's death.

"Please let me live," he murmured humbly over and over again.

Leif did not stop running until he was near the beach, where he was sure the ice was thick enough to carry him. On the beach Odd, Flose, and Atle stood waiting.

"Egil is dead," he declared — rather unnecessarily, for the others had clearly seen what had happened.

"Now Brattahlid is yours." Odd's voice trembled a little as he looked up at the hall that had once belonged to Erik the Red.

"Mine?" Leif shook his head.

"Yes, you are our chieftain." Flose pounded the end of his spear upon the pebbles.

"Where is Bera?" Leif looked about, expecting the girl to be near.

"I told her of Ingeborg's death, I think she went to seek her. You will find her" — Atle paused a moment — "in your hall." He stepped aside to let Leif pass.

"Thank you." Leif nodded to Atle. He wanted badly to speak to Bera, to talk with her. He felt that she alone would understand him, would believe him when he said that he had not wished any of what had happened. Yet he tarried, feeling that there was something else he needed to do first. He unfastened his belt, loosening the sword and scabbard. Handing the weapon to Odd, he said, "You carry it, and may it never be unsheathed again." Then he walked up toward the hall, where he knew he would find Bera. There was so much to do, both now and in the future. He was chieftain of Brattahlid, ruler of the Norsemen in Greenland. In the northern sky great banks of clouds were building, promising the first real winter snowfall.